The Scarred Double Eagle

The Scarred Double Eagle

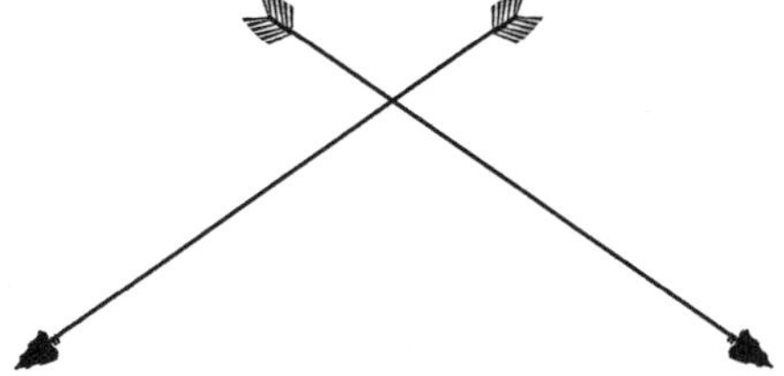

Donald P. Gregg

SHIRES PRESS
4869 Main Street
P.O. Box 2200
Manchester Center, VT 05255
www.northshire.com

The Scarred Double Eagle

ISBN: 978-1-60571-334-2

Building Community, One Book at a Time
A family-owned, independent bookstore in
Manchester Ctr., VT, since 1976 and Saratoga Springs, NY since 2013.
We are committed to excellence in bookselling.
The Northshire Bookstore's mission is to serve as a resource for
information, ideas, and entertainment while honoring the needs
of customers, staff, and community.

Printed in the United States of America

For my grandchildren,
Cat, Conor, Gregg, Alex,
Meggie and Tyquan:
I hope you will enjoy this book
and pass it on to your children.

Contents

Foreword

A major source for material in *The Scarred Double Eagle* was my grandfather, Harry Renick Gregg, who lived from 1852 to 1950. My last conversation with him was in late June of 1950, when we talked about the Civil War, which he remembered clearly. He told me that as a boy of 12, he had seen President Lincoln's funeral train pass through Circleville, Ohio, and said to me, "The sadness and the silence were unforgettable".

Grandfather Gregg sent me two silver dollars every Christmas, which I would find under my plate at breakfast on Christmas morning. Some were quite old, and I remember wondering whose hands they had passed through and how they had been spent. My grandfather had a great sense of humor, and was particularly fond of stories about a horse named Jenny. He also spilled hot coffee into saucers to make it easier to drink.

He lived through difficult times in Ohio, Texas and Colorado, but kept his cheerful perspective right up to his death, just short of his 99th birthday. I try to bring him alive in Great Uncle Harry, and to tell part of the story of one twenty-dollar gold piece, called a double eagle, whose scarred face hints at the difficulties of those days on the western frontier.

Donald P. Gregg

Prologue – 1866

Say Your Prayers and Be Ready to Die

Sam Pickett lay spread-eagled in a Crow Indian lodge. His wrists were tied to stakes driven deep into the hard-packed floor. In the center of the lodge a small fire burned. On the other side of the fire sat an old woman, sharpening a long knife and humming a tribal song. Outside the lodge, by a larger fire, sat Crow warriors. Sam could hear the rise and fall of their voices as they argued over his fate.

Sam's head ached, his beard itched and he was desperately hungry. He raised his head and looked at the old woman with what he hoped was a charming smile. She drew the edge of the knife across her throat.

Sam lowered his head and thought hard about his situation. That morning, while setting beaver traps in a stream, Sam had been caught by a war party of Crow braves. The Crows had waited until Sam put down his rifle, picked up a trap and waded into the stream. Four of them surrounded him - two with rifles and two with bows and arrows. Sam knew from their dress that they were Crow, and spoke to them in their tongue. This surprised the braves, and probably saved Sam's life.

Sam said, "I am a friend of your people; I have lived among you. I come in peace." The warriors looked at each other in doubt. Sam spoke again, "I have lived in the lodge of Broken Lance, and I have shared the hunger of the winter of great snows with your people."

This was true. Two years before, Sam was caught in the high mountains by an early snow. He had struggled down to a warmer valley where a branch of the Crow tribe wintered. They shared their food with him, and he helped them through a hard winter by using his skill as a hunter, and his accurate long rifle, to kill game. Sam believed that the Crow were his friends, and for that reason had returned to their land to trap beaver. However, the war party that had captured Sam was from a different branch of the Crow tribe. To make matters worse, the war party was returning empty-handed from a horse raid on a Sioux village, and Sam was something to take back to their village, to show their skill and bravery.

Sam had decided that his best chance was to go peacefully with the war party. The braves divided his possessions among themselves. Around his neck, Sam wore a newly-minted twenty dollar gold piece called a double eagle, as a good luck charm. One of the braves ripped the coin from Sam's neck, breaking the thong on which it hung, hurting his neck in the process. At that moment, Sam decided that he had a score to settle with that brave, who had a big nose and eyes set close together.

The Indians put one of Sam's own ropes around his neck and allowed him to mount his horse. Then they tied his hands behind him. Big Nose (Sam's name for the brave who had stolen his double eagle) held the end of the rope and jerked it frequently to remind Sam that he was captive.

The braves rode all day, stopping only once at noon. They offered Sam nothing to eat, but allowed him to drink from a stream where they crossed at a shallow ford. Sam noted that there were many smooth stones about the size of chicken eggs, lying three or four inches beneath the surface of the water. An hour's ride beyond the stream, the braves stopped and applied war paint to their faces. Remounting their horses, they galloped over a ridge and down to their village. The warriors whooped and yelled as they rode into the circle of buffalo-skin lodges, and the women and children of the village ran out to greet them. The women quickly noted that all of the braves had returned from the war party, and their cries of greeting were joyful. They crowded around the warriors, and listened as Big Nose boasted of his own bravery in capturing Sam. Sam had two riding horses and three pack mules, in addition to his rifles, traps and food; his capture had made the war party a success.

Sam looked for familiar faces among the Indians crowding around him; he saw none. He noticed a dignified older warrior standing in front of the most elaborately-painted lodge, and guessed that he was the chief of the village. Sam was pulled off of his horse and led to a lodge at the edge of the village. There, he was staked to the floor and left to his own thoughts.

Suddenly, four Indians entered the lodge, stooping as they pushed aside the flap that covered the lodge's only opening. First came the older warrior whom Sam had seen earlier standing by his lodge. Then came Big Nose and two of the other young braves from the war party. Big Nose now wore Sam's double eagle around his neck. The four stood, looking down at Sam in silence. Sam spoke first, in the Crow tongue. "I come in peace to your land. On my pack mules are presents for your people. I have lived among you. I call Broken Lance my friend. I do not understand this strange greeting that your braves have given me."

Big Nose retorted angrily, "He comes to kill our beaver. He is the scout for many other white men who will come with disease and whiskey. They will take our land, they will kill all the animals and leave us nothing. The tribes to the east know this to be true."

The chief then spoke to Sam and asked, "Are you the one they call Red Beard?"

"That is the name given to me by Broken Lance and his family, yes," said Sam.

"I have heard of you," said the chief. "You understand our ways and have lived among us. But where you come, many other white men will follow. What he says is true," said the chief, nodding his head toward Big Nose, who sneered at Sam.

Sam felt his fate slipping from his control, so he spoke with great intensity. "I tell the white men about the Crow people. I tell them that you are different from the Sioux and the Blackfeet. You do not fight the white man, you wish to live in peace and you deserve to have your wish. If you kill me, your message will be lost." The Indians looked at each other, and Sam knew that his words had made an impression.

The chief looked hard at Sam and said, "We will talk more."

As the Indians turned to leave, Sam spoke once more, "I thank you for the hospitality of this lodge, but ask that I be allowed to step into the bushes for a moment, as I do not wish to offend the women of this tent by doing inside what should only be done outside."

Sam thought that he saw a faint smile on the chief's face as he ordered Big Nose to allow Sam to go outside. With the rope still around his neck, Sam was allowed to walk to some bushes to relieve himself. He returned to the tent, feeling much better, and before being staked to the floor, was given some dried buffalo meat to eat. Sam took these gestures as encouraging signs, and was able to sleep.

Deep in the night, Sam was awakened by a kick in his ribs. An Indian leaned down and whispered harshly in his ear, "In the morning, we will let you run. Four braves will pursue you - two who run fast and two who run far. I tell you this so that you can say your prayers to the white man's god, and be ready to die."

Sam could not see the face of the Indian who whispered to him, but his breath stank and his tone was cruel. Sam guessed that it was Big Nose. To deceive Big Nose, Sam pretended to be afraid and asked, in a trembling voice, to be allowed to speak to the chief. The Indian laughed and left the lodge without speaking.

Sam thought about this. He was not ready to die. His heart was full of hope - he knew that his legs were strong and, in a secret place, perhaps two hours' run from the village, Sam had hidden a small cache of food and a loaded pistol. He smiled in the darkness.

Chapter 1

1921 – Great Uncle Harry Arrives

"Your Great Uncle Harry is coming to spend Christmas with us," said Mrs. Corliss at dinner one evening, early in December. Elizabeth, who was nine at the time, was chewing on a rather tough piece of roast beef, so she made no comment in reply. Her older brother, Tom, was trying to hide a very tough piece of the same roast beef under a lettuce leaf. He, too, made no reply.

Mr. Corliss, knowing that Elizabeth thought that horses were more interesting than people, said, "Great Uncle Harry raises horses on a ranch in Wyoming."

This got Elizabeth's attention, and she asked, "How many horses are on his ranch, and what kind are they?" She was told that her great uncle kept about 200 horses at one time, and that he sold them to dude ranches and stockmen. Elizabeth, who dreamed one day of having her own horse, assumed a look of great concentration, and continued to chew.

Tom asked for more mashed potatoes, and his mother plopped the new serving directly on top of the gristly roast beef. She looked at Tom with a secret smile as she passed him his plate. Tom had a strong interest in cowboys and Indians, and asked if Uncle Harry had many cowboys working for him. Neither Mr. nor Mrs. Corliss knew the answer to that question, as Great Uncle Harry had always been a somewhat remote and mysterious figure who rarely left Wyoming.

Elizabeth, still looking very serious, asked what Great Uncle Harry did with the horses that he could not sell, or horses that were too small for work with cowboys or dude ranches. Her mother told her that that would be a very good question to ask Great Uncle Harry when he came to visit.

"What is a great uncle?" asked Tom.

"Harry is your Grandfather Frank's older brother," said Mrs. Corliss. Tom and Elizabeth knew about Grandfather Frank. He was their mother's father who lived in Boston. He sometimes came to visit the Corliss family. His wife, Mary, had been a great beauty as a young woman, and Elizabeth hoped that she would one day grow up to look like her grandmother.

Elizabeth asked if Great Uncle Harry had a wife, and was told that he had never married.

"Why?" asked Elizabeth.

Mrs. Corliss looked at her husband, and there was silence around the table.

"I guess he never found a woman he wanted to marry who wanted to marry him," said Mr. Corliss.

"That's sad," said Elizabeth, who thought that everyone should be married and live happily ever after.

"Does he have any other family?" asked Tom.

"I guess we are as close to him as anyone is," said Mrs. Corliss.

"Maybe he didn't want to be alone at Christmas," Elizabeth ventured.

"I think that's right," said Mr. Corliss. "We've written to him for several years, inviting him to come for a visit. This year, he said he'd be glad to come, because a lot of his friends have been moving on, and it's getting a bit lonely at his ranch."

"How old is he?" asked Tom.

"I think he's about eighty, but I'm not sure," said Mrs. Corliss.

"That's very old," said Elizabeth.

"I think you'll forget how old he is when you see him," said her father.

Chapter 2

Many Questions, Few Answers

Great Uncle Harry was due to arrive by train on Christmas Eve. Elizabeth knew what time the train came in, and how long it took a taxi to climb slowly up the steep hill to the Corliss home. She waited on the living room floor, with her chin on a window sill. Her braids hung down her back as she looked out across the front porch, down the front steps to the curb where the taxi would come. She thought about horses, and imagined Great Uncle Harry riding up to her front door on a great black stallion, leading a pinto pony just for her. Instead, she saw a creaky old black taxi pull up to her house.

After what seemed like a long time, the back door of the taxi opened and a long leg appeared. The taxi rocked on its springs as a tall man squeezed out of the door. In one hand, he held a black hat with a broad brim, and in the other, a dark leather satchel of considerable size. Elizabeth thought that she had never seen a man so tall, and watched as he put on his hat, closed the door of the taxi and strode slowly toward the house.

Mrs. Corliss had also been waiting at the door. She met the tall man at the top of the porch steps. "Hello, Uncle Harry, how good to see you!" she said.

Elizabeth's Great Uncle Harry climbed to the top of the stairs and took off his hat. He towered over his niece. Putting down his satchel, he took her extended hand and shook it quite formally, looking steadily into her upturned face. Great Uncle Harry had a full head of gray hair and a walrus mustache, more white than gray. His eyes were dark and deep-set. Elizabeth stood shyly by the door, her hands clasped behind her back. Her great uncle turned and looked at Elizabeth. She felt the impact of his eyes. "And who is this?" asked Great Uncle Harry, in a deep voice.

"This is Elizabeth," said Mrs. Corliss.

Elizabeth stepped forward and performed a rather awkward curtsy. It was hard to keep her balance while looking up at Great Uncle Harry's face. He smiled down at her and shook her hand. "You look just like your grandma," he said. Nothing could have pleased Elizabeth more, and she beamed.

Inside the house, Elizabeth held Great Uncle Harry's hat as he removed his long black coat, which reached well below his knees. His suit and vest were black, and he wore a fresh white shirt with a narrow string tie. On his feet were high-heeled cowboy boots, which added to his great height. From a pocket in his vest hung a golden coin, on the end of a watch fob. Elizabeth had never seen such a coin, and was immediately curious about it.

Mrs. Corliss led the way upstairs to the guest room, and Elizabeth followed, not wanting to miss a word. Tom came running in from a game of football with the neighborhood boys. He immediately asked Great Uncle Harry about all manner of Western things: guns, Indians, snakes, cowboys, bears, catamounts, saloons and round-ups. Great Uncle Harry answered the questions, but not in much detail. Tom was a bit disappointed, and said later to his mother that, for someone who had lived in the West, Great Uncle Harry did not seem to know much about what had been going on. Mrs. Corliss smiled and said that, as Great Uncle Harry got to know the family better, perhaps he would talk more freely.

The evening was busy with the last-minute wrapping of packages and the filling of stockings. Great Uncle Harry sat quietly smoking a pipe, which filled the house with a fragrance that set Elizabeth to thinking of far-away places she hoped one day to see.

Before she went to bed, Elizabeth went over to Great Uncle Harry and patted him on his arm. "I'm so glad that you came for Christmas," she said.

"So am I," said Great Uncle Harry, as he gave Elizabeth a hug.

Great Uncle Harry

Chapter 3

Silver Dollars and History

The presents had all been opened, and the Corliss family was about to sit down to Christmas dinner. Elizabeth was pleased with her gifts, but one thing bothered her - Great Uncle Harry had not given her or her brother a present. He had given her mother a Navajo necklace made of turquoise and silver, and her father a hand-tooled belt with a silver buckle, but nothing for the children. Elizabeth was annoyed at Great Uncle Harry, but also embarrassed for him. Perhaps, she thought, because he never married, he doesn't know about giving presents to children at Christmas.

Elizabeth looked at Great Uncle Harry with a slight frown on her face. He looked back at her with an expression that she could not read. Elizabeth thought of the linen handkerchief she had given him, and how hard she had worked to sew the letter "H" onto one corner of it. She felt quite resentful as she sat down to dinner. While her father said grace, Elizabeth looked at Tom, and guessed from his expression that he felt the same way.

Mr. Corliss finished grace and rose to carve the turkey. Great Uncle Harry was served first, then Mrs. Corliss and then Elizabeth. Her father cut a generous piece for Elizabeth and asked her to pass her plate. As Elizabeth lifted her plate, she saw three large silver coins, arranged in a neat triangle, hidden underneath.

"What are these?" asked Elizabeth, surprised.

Tom snatched up his plate and found three coins waiting for him. Great Uncle Harry sat with his arms folded, puffing at his pipe.

Elizabeth looked more closely at her coins. They were silver dollars. One was bright and shiny, dated 1921. The other two were rather dingy and gray, and in a different design. Elizabeth preferred the bright and shiny new coin. She quickly looked at Tom's coins and saw that he had two shiny new silver dollars, and only one dingy gray one. Elizabeth was about to complain loudly about this when her mother spoke gently, saying, "The coins are from Great Uncle Harry. He brought them especially for you from Wyoming."

"Thank you very much, Great Uncle Harry," said Tom enthusiastically.

"Thank you, Great Uncle Harry," said Elizabeth in a subdued voice.

Tom knew what was bothering Elizabeth, and he smirked at her. Elizabeth stuck her tongue out at her brother, and tried to kick him under the table.

Great Uncle Harry observed all this through a cloud of tobacco smoke. Putting down his pipe, he looked directly at Elizabeth and asked, "Which coin do you like best?"

Elizabeth thought that a very odd question, and hesitated before answering. Tom, enjoying the moment, blurted out, "I like my two new ones best."

Great Uncle Harry turned his heavy gaze on Tom and said, "That surprises me, Tom. Why do you like the new ones, is it because they are shiny?" Great Uncle Harry's words were gentle, but carried humor with them.

Tom was at a loss for words, knowing that he had blundered into a kind of trap, but not knowing how to get out of it. Elizabeth's mind was racing, trying to grasp what Great Uncle Harry was getting at, knowing that he was testing her, and that she was failing. Great Uncle Harry came to the rescue of both children. Reaching into an inner pocket of his coat, he brought out a stack of silver dollars, which chinked pleasantly in his fingers. He placed three shiny coins to one side saying "These are new, you can trade for them if you'd like."

He took the other coins and read the dates aloud, "1914, the year the World War started; 1865, the year the Civil War ended; 1902, the year I bought my ranch in Wyoming; 1862, the year I first crossed the Missouri River."

Turning to Elizabeth, Great Uncle Harry asked "What are the dates on your old coins?"

Elizabeth read the dates aloud in a small voice, "1870 and 1908."

"How about your old coin, Tom?" said Great Uncle Harry.

"Mine is dated 1876," answered Tom.

"Those are all significant dates for me, said Great Uncle Harry. "1870 was the first year I met your Grandma; 1876 was the year that General Custer got massacred by the Sioux; and 1908 was the year your mother and father got married." He paused and took out his watch. He held the watch, letting the gold coin attached to it swing beneath his hand. "I like looking at an old coin and thinking of the year it was minted - remembering where I was that year, and wondering who all the people were who ever held the coin, what they purchased, and whether the people were happy or sad about what they bought." Great Uncle Harry stopped speaking and puffed on his pipe.

Tears were in Elizabeth's eyes, but she didn't quite know why. She slipped from her chair and went around the table to Great Uncle Harry. Putting her cheek against his shoulder, she said, "Thank you, Great Uncle Harry. I love my coins and the dates on them. I'd like to keep the new one, because it's the year I first met you."

Great Uncle Harry put his arm around Elizabeth and hugged her close. "That truly pleases me, Elizabeth," he said.

Elizabeth went to bed soon afterward, and slept with the silver dollars under her pillow. She dreamed of faraway places, and lands she had never known.

Tom, who could stay up later than Elizabeth, looked up General Custer in the encyclopedia. He read about "Little Big Horn", "Sitting Bull" and the other entries he was led to by the encyclopedia's index.

He was sitting at the kitchen table, encyclopedia open before him and his mind filled with thoughts of Custer's bloody defeat, when Great Uncle Harry came in and asked what he was doing. Tom said he was doing "research" on General Custer, and Great Uncle Harry remarked that Custer was a man about whom much would be written for many years to come.

"Did you know him?" asked Tom.

"I saw him parading around a few times," said Great Uncle Harry, in a faintly disapproving tone. He added, "Custer is a man worth thinking about; you can learn a lot from his mistakes. I'm glad that old silver dollar got you started on your research."

"I am, too" said Tom. "I wonder where this coin was on the day Custer was defeated?"

"That's a good thing to wonder about," said Great Uncle Harry, as he walked out of the kitchen, trailing tobacco smoke behind him.

Tom followed him into the hall, and said that he had a question to ask.

"What is it, Tom?" asked Great Uncle Harry.

"I was wondering if I could trade my two new silver dollars for two of those old ones you have in your coat pocket."

"I think we could arrange that," said Great Uncle Harry, "Which ones would you like instead?"

"I'd like the two oldest ones," said Tom.

Great Uncle Harry fished the silver dollars out of his pocket and found the two oldest coins. An exchange was made at the foot of the stairs, and Tom ran off to bed. Great Uncle Harry smiled as he watched him go.

Harry returned to the living room and sat before the dying embers of the fire. He pulled his watch from his vest pocket and let the gold coin swing back and forth, its worn surface catching the light of the fire, gently reflecting it back to his eye. Before putting his watch away, Great Uncle Harry looked intently at the coin and ran his fingernail over the primitive design gouged into its face. He rose, went out the front door and onto the porch. The night was cold and a wind had swept the sky, leaving the stars shining brightly. Great Uncle Harry located the Big Dipper, and from it the North Star. He turned and looked to the west, toward his ranch, the mountains and his memories.

Chapter 4

Spilled Coffee

Early the next morning, Elizabeth bounded down the stairs, looking for Great Uncle Harry. She was disappointed to find that he had not yet appeared. Mrs. Corliss was in the kitchen preparing breakfast. "Where's Great Uncle Harry?" asked Elizabeth.

"I heard him moving around upstairs. Why don't you take him a cup of coffee?" suggested Mrs. Corliss.

Elizabeth took a cup of coffee upstairs and tried her best not to spill it. Despite her best efforts, quite a lot of coffee had spilled out of the cup into the saucer beneath it. Elizabeth put the coffee on the floor outside

Great Uncle Harry's room, and knocked rather timidly on the door. "Come in," said Great Uncle Harry.

Elizabeth opened the door and saw Great Uncle Harry putting on his tie, standing in front of a mirror. "I brought you some coffee, but I spilled a lot of it," said Elizabeth sheepishly.

Great Uncle Harry watched as Elizabeth carried the cup and saucer over to him. "That's just fine, Elizabeth," said Great Uncle Harry, to make her feel better. "I always pour coffee into the saucer to cool it before I drink."

Elizabeth watched Great Uncle Harry as he took the cup in one hand and the saucer in the other. He carefully sipped the spilled coffee in the saucer, said that the temperature was just fine, and poured the remainder back into the cup. He looked at Elizabeth with one of those expressions that she could not understand.

"Are you teasing me?" asked Elizabeth.

"Certainly not," said Great Uncle Harry, as he finished adjusting his tie. He picked up his vest. As he did so, Elizabeth saw the gold coin flash in the light.

"Would you please tell me about the coin that's tied to your watch?" asked Elizabeth.

Great Uncle Harry handed her his watch, fob and coin. "That's a twenty dollar gold piece. It's called a 'double eagle'," said Great Uncle Harry.

"Why is it called that?" asked Elizabeth.

"Well, a ten dollar gold piece is called an 'eagle', and this one is worth double that," said Great Uncle Harry.

"It does have an eagle on it," noted Elizabeth.

"That probably has something to do with it," said Great Uncle Harry, winking.

Elizabeth looked hard at the coin and noticed that something was cut into its surface. "What is this scratched on the coin?" she asked. "It looks like a tadpole."

"That's the sign of Broken Lance, a famous Crow Indian chief, and he'd be highly offended to hear you call his sign a tadpole," said Great Uncle Harry, smiling at Elizabeth.

"Well, that's what it looks like to me," said Elizabeth firmly. "Why did he do that?" she asked.

Great Uncle Harry put on his coat and paused before he answered. "That's a long story, Elizabeth, and it's just a small part of the history of that old double eagle."

"Will you tell me about it?" asked Elizabeth.

"I'd be pleased to," said Great Uncle Harry.

"When?" asked Elizabeth.

"How about tonight after supper, just before you go to bed?" suggested Great Uncle Harry.

"That would be wonderful!" said Elizabeth, as she took Great Uncle Harry's hand and led him down to breakfast. "I can hardly wait."

Chapter 5

The Runningest, Jumpingest Man I Ever Saw

Supper was finished, and Elizabeth sat beside Great Uncle Harry on the couch in front of the fire. Tom hung back a little, curious, yet unsure. "You're welcome to listen, Tom," said Great Uncle Harry. "You may find that some of this bears directly on those questions you asked me the other day." Tom perched on the edge of his chair, and looked into the fire as Great Uncle Harry began to speak.

"The first man who had this coin was Sam Pickett. He was a wild mountain man and trapper, six and a half feet tall, with a red beard and hair to match. He looked skinny as a rail, but was strong as a bull. He was the runningest, jumpingest man I ever saw, and besides that, he could walk on his hands. He was a dead shot with a rifle, and could split a shingle at twenty paces with a thrown hatchet or a Bowie knife. He could outrun and outwrestle any man, with the possible exception of me." Great Uncle Harry paused for effect.

"Could you beat him at wrestling, Great Uncle Harry?" asked Tom.

Great Uncle Harry cleared his throat. "Well, I'm left-handed, as you may have noticed, and Sam was right-handed. I could beat Sam arm-wrestling left-handed, and he could beat me right-handed. Sam liked me, but it really surprised him that anybody could beat him at anything. Three or four times a year, Sam would come into the trading post where I worked. He'd ride in, bragging about how he had been building up his left arm so that he could beat me. He'd attract a big crowd, and bets would be made before we started. We'd always start right-handed and Sam would beat me, but not without a struggle. Then, after a lot of bragging and swaggering around, we'd go at it left-handed. I always managed to win, but once it took thirty minutes. You never heard such hollering and betting and carrying-on! After I'd forced his wrist down, Sam looked at me and said, 'Well, Lefty, I guess God made you the way you are just to show the world that I ain't perfect.' Everybody laughed and stomped around, and it was a good time."

"What about the double eagle?" Elizabeth asked gently.

"Sam would bring his beaver pelts in to the post in the spring. He would take his pay partly in trade goods, partly in cash. One year, we had some new double eagles, and Sam like the design. He drilled a hole in one of them and wore it around his neck, on a thong. Here's the hole right here; I still use it to attach the coin to the watch fob."

"And then what happened?" asked Elizabeth.

"Well, Sam got a little careless that year, and let some young Crow bucks sneak up on him while he was setting a trap in a creek. Sam knew some Crow and spoke their language, but this was a different group of Crows. Some wanted to kill him and some wanted to let him go, so they split the difference - they decided to let Sam run for his life, and they sent four braves after him."

Sam Pickett's pursurers

Chapter 6

A Run for His Life

At dawn, the Crows untied Sam and led him out of the lodge. He was stiff, and bounced up and down on his haunches to loosen his muscles.

The chief of the village spoke to him. "We will let you run back toward where you came from, Red Beard. If you can out-run my warriors, you may live; if they catch you, you may die."

Sam saw four braves, stripped to their breechcloths and moccasins. One of them was Big Nose, who grinned wolfishly at Sam. All four Indians carried war clubs. One brave, who looked younger than the rest, also carried what looked to be a short spear. He wore no feathers in his hair, indicating that he had never counted coup on an enemy. Sam's name for him was "No Feathers."

"How much of a head start do I get?" asked Sam.

"As far as you can throw a stone," the chief replied.

Sam picked up a smooth, rounded stone from the ground. Holding it in his hand, he looked at each of his pursuers. Big Nose shook his war club at Sam, while the other three stood by impassively.

"I'm ready," said Sam, and threw the stone far up the slope.

The Indians grunted in surprise at the distance of Sam's throw. Sam slowly began to walk up the slope. He took deep breaths and tried to compose himself for what was to come. He looked over his shoulder at the Indians below. Well before he reached the place where the stone had landed, Big Nose shouted something and started running. The others followed behind. Sam broke into a long, loping run and quickly reached the top of the ridge. Glancing back, Sam saw that Big Nose and another stocky brave were about 200 feet behind him. Another 100 feet back were No Feathers and the other brave - both running, like Sam, with long, easy strides.

Sam headed for the stone-filled stream where the Crows had let him drink the day before. He found his pace and was running easily, but Big Nose was slowly gaining. The second Indian had fallen 50 feet behind. As he ran, Sam developed a plan to survive. His goal was to get to his cache, which held his loaded pistol.

Before he reached it, he knew that he would have to stop Big Nose and the other fast runner.

Thirty minutes later, Sam saw the cottonwood trees along the bank of the stream. Big Nose had continued to gain on him, and he was now only about 100 feet behind. Sam sprinted toward the stream to gain distance and time. Dashing into the water, Sam bent down. With one hand he splashed water into his mouth, and with the other, he picked up two rounded stones from the streambed. Sam heard Big Nose rushing after him, so he darted across the stream and up the bank on the far side.

Now less than 20 feet behind, Big Nose lunged after Sam. Sam shifted one of the stones into his left hand. Reaching a flat piece of ground where the footing was certain, Sam whirled, got his balance and threw the stone, striking Big Nose in the pit of his stomach. Big Nose grunted and fell to his hands and knees. Sam leapt upon him and tore the war club from his grasp. With one sweeping blow, Sam struck one of Big Nose's legs, and then turned to face the second Crow warrior. The Indian stopped 15 feet from Sam, and looked back at the two long-runners; they were only 100 yards away. The Indian decided to wait for reinforcements. Sam held the war club in his right hand and the second stone in his left. Raising his left arm, he awkwardly threw the stone at the Indian closest to him, in a high, lazy arc. The Crow raised his eyes to watch the stone, and Sam hurled the war club directly at him. The head of the club smashed the

Sam Pickett stops Big Nose with a thrown stone

Crow brave's shoulder, and he cried out in pain. Sam turned and ran, knowing that now he had only two pursuers to deal with.

"I think it's about time for you to go to bed, Elizabeth," said Great Uncle Harry.

"No!" wailed Elizabeth, from underneath the couch cushion she had pulled over her head. Tom sat in his chair, staring wide-eyed at Great Uncle Harry.

In the doorway, Mrs. Corliss said, "I think you'd better get Sam safely out of this scrape, so we all can sleep soundly tonight." With her permission, Great Uncle Harry resumed his story.

As Sam ran on, he visualized the lay of the land around his cache. He had found a small, dry cave near the top of an oddly-shaped butte, easy to spot from afar. Inside the cave, Sam had hidden a parfleche filled with pemmican, and a cap and ball pistol wrapped in a piece of canvas. Sam figured that he would need at least a minute to pull away the stones with which he had blocked the entrance to the cave, then to open the parfleche and unwrap the pistol. He had stored the cache only two weeks earlier, so he was quite certain that the pistol would fire; his problem was time.

The two long-runners were easily keeping up with him. They were running smoothly, side by side, about 100 yards behind him. Looking ahead, Sam saw the outline of the butte where his cache lay. The entrance to the cave was on a narrow ledge. Below the ledge, a steep and rock-strewn slope dropped down to the prairie floor. Sam ran toward the butte so as to approach the foot of the slope directly below the cave.

As he reached the bottom of the butte, Sam sensed that the Indians had quickened their pace and were gaining on him. He threw himself up the slope, scrambling desperately to keep ahead of his pursuers. He heard them close behind. Grabbing a loose rock, he turned and hurled it down the slope. Only one Indian, No Feathers, pursued him. The other was circling, knowing that the butte was easier to climb on its far side. Sam spotted another loose rock and heaved it at No Feathers. The young brave saw it coming and ducked under Sam's throw. Sam grabbed yet another stone and hurled it downward. This time his aim was better. The stone struck the youth's leg, and he cried out in pain.

Sam pulled himself up on the ledge, and saw the entrance to his cave a few feet to his right. He rushed to the cave and tore away the stones that he had piled at the entrance. No Feathers was still coming, so Sam threw the stones down at him. He scored no hits, and the young Indian kept climbing. Sam thrust himself into the cave and saw the parfleche, sitting just as he had left it. Sam ripped it open and grabbed the pistol. As he did so, the second Indian jumped down from above the cave and leaped at him, swinging his club. Sam pushed the parfleche forward as a shield and it absorbed some of the blow. Sam was knocked backward, onto the cave's floor. The Indian was crouched for another blow at Sam, when Sam pulled the pistol free. "Hold it!" shouted Sam. The Indian, never hesitating, jumped forward, swinging his club at Sam's head. Sam fired, and the Indian reeled back, holding his shoulder. Sam kicked the war club away from the Indian, and stepped out of the cave. No Feathers was just pulling himself onto the ledge.

Sam moved away from the entrance of the cave, fearing that the wounded Indian might come at him again. No Feathers stood on the ledge. He held his war club in one hand, and a long coup stick in the other.

Sam pointed his pistol at No Feathers, and said, in his most stern voice "I don't want to kill you, boy."

No Feathers looked at Sam with a fatal sadness in his eyes and said, "I cannot run from you, Red Beard. You know that. You know our people, you know our customs."

And so the two faced each other, on a narrow ledge high above the plains. Sam cocked his pistol, and pointed it at No Feathers' head. At the same time, Sam drew back his left hand, which held the pistol, and extended his right hand, with the fist clenched. No Feathers stared at Sam, but could read nothing in his eyes. The young Indian edged forward from the ledge, his coup stick extended, his war club ready. The muzzle of Sam's pistol looked like the black eye of death to No Feathers, but still he moved forward until he was able to strike Sam's right wrist sharply with his coup stick. "I count coup on you, Red Beard," said No Feathers.

Sam lowered his pistol. "Well counted," he said, and made the sign of peace with his right hand.

No Feathers stepped back and made the sign of peace.

"Let us see how your friend is doing in the cave," said Sam.

Both men laid down their weapons, and moved to tend the wounded Indian in the cave. The shadow of death lifted from the butte.

Elizabeth was bursting with questions, "What's a parfleche? What's pemmican? What is counting coup? Did Big Nose die? What happened to the double eagle?"

Mrs. Corliss sat beside Elizabeth and put her arms around her daughter. She could feel her heart pounding with excitement. Mrs. Corliss looked at Great Uncle Harry and raised her eyebrows. "Uncle Harry, she's about to explode!" said Mrs. Corliss.

Great Uncle Harry reached out and took Elizabeth's face in his great hand. "Elizabeth," he said, "I'm telling you a happy story. Sam liked the Crow Indians. He wanted to be at peace with them. No one died. He and No Feathers became friends. It turned out all right."

Elizabeth sighed and rubbed her eyes with her fists. "I was afraid for everybody," she said.

Great Uncle Harry took her hand and led Elizabeth upstairs to bed.

Chapter 7

Bad Dreams and Good Memories

Elizabeth was having a bad dream. She was among a tribe of fierce Indians who did not like the doll that she was carrying. Elizabeth loved the doll, and tried to explain to the Indians how nice and friendly it was, but they would not believe her. The fiercest Indian kept trying to reach out and grab the doll, so Elizabeth kept turning away from him. Suddenly, the Indian seized her shoulder, and at that point she woke up. Usually, when Elizabeth had a bad dream, she would quietly slip into bed beside her mother, where she knew that she would be safe and sound. She immediately got out of her bed, and headed for the door to her parents' room.

Elizabeth passed the head of the stairs and saw that there was still a light on in the living room. Peeking down through the bannister rails, she saw that Great Uncle Harry was still sitting in front of the fire, smoking his pipe. Since she felt that it was his fault that she had had a bad dream, Elizabeth went downstairs to tell Great Uncle Harry about it. Great Uncle Harry heard Elizabeth sniffling as she came down the stairs. He seemed to know what had happened. "Did you have a bad dream?" he asked gently.

"Yes!" said Elizabeth. "It was all about bad Indians. It was awful."

"Well, sit here beside me until you feel better about things," said Great Uncle Harry.

Elizabeth snuggled beside Great Uncle Harry on the couch, and he put his arm around her.

"There *were* some bad Indians, but most of the ones that I knew were brave and honest, and true friends," said Great Uncle Harry.

"Tell me about some Indians like that," begged Elizabeth.

"Well, the best way to do that is to tell you some more about Sam Pickett and his adventures," said Great Uncle Harry. "I was riding my horse outside the trading post one evening, just admiring the sunset and the beauty of nature, when I saw a tall figure loping toward me over the plains. I soon recognized Sam, but couldn't believe my eyes. The last time I had seen him, he was riding out to trap beaver with horses, mules, guns, traps and blankets. And here he came on foot, carrying a pistol in one hand and an empty parfleche in the other.

"'Hello, Lefty, was you out looking for me?' said Sam cheerfully as he saw who I was."

"I could see that Sam was tired and worn thin, so I got off my horse and let him ride in to the post. Sam told me what had happened to him. He seemed both angry and curious. He could not understand why the Crows had treated him so badly. I told Sam I thought that he was lucky to be alive."

"'The more you plan ahead, the more luck you have,' said Sam seriously, looking down at me as I walked beside the horse. 'I have four or five other caches hidden around this territory. You never know when you may need help in a hurry. I may have been able to outrun those last two Indians, but maybe not. And if they'd have caught me, I'd have had to kill them, or they'd have killed me. This way, we're all alive, and that's good.'" Great Uncle Harry looked down to see if Elizabeth was still awake. She was.

"What happened to No Feathers and the one who was shot?" she asked.

"After Sam and No Feathers had made peace out on the ledge, they went into the cave and found that the other Indian, who was called One Buck, was unconscious and bleeding badly from the wound in his shoulder. Sam used the canvas that had been wrapped around the pistol to make a kind of bandage to stop the bleeding. The next day, when One Buck was feeling a little stronger, they moved down to the bank of a stream, where Sam could wash the wound. The three of them spent another day there, and then Sam gave them half of what was left of the pemmican. The Indians headed back for their village, and Sam started to walk toward the trading post. He said he had gotten to know One Buck and No Feathers very well, and that they had become friends. They all knew that they had come through a hard test, and that all of them had done well. None of them had anything to be ashamed of. That was important to Sam, and important to those Indians as well. Sam felt good about that part of his story, but he was mad at Big Nose."

"Why?" asked Elizabeth.

"I guess the thing that Sam objected to most was the fact that Big Nose had stolen his double eagle. He was determined to get that back, along with the rest of his gear," said Great Uncle Harry.

"Did he ever get it back?" asked Elizabeth, in a sleepy voice.

"I'll tell you that tomorrow," said Great Uncle Harry, and for the second time that night he led Elizabeth upstairs to bed.

"What if I have another bad dream?" asked Elizabeth, after Great Uncle Harry had tucked her into bed.

"I'll sit here and make sure that you don't," said Great Uncle Harry, lowering himself into a rocking chair near Elizabeth's bed.

"Thank you, Great Uncle Harry," said Elizabeth, almost asleep.

The room became quiet, except for the creak of the old rocker. Elizabeth slept peacefully, and did not hear Great Uncle Harry as he rose quietly from the chair. After looking intently at her for a moment, he smiled and went down the hall to his own room.

Chapter 8

Saladin Meets His Match

The next morning was bright and sunny, and unusually warm for late December. At breakfast, Elizabeth raised the subject of horses, said proudly that she had taken riding lessons at a stable, and that she hoped to have a horse of her own one day.

"Well, I'd certainly like to see you on a horse," said Great Uncle Harry. "Do you do any riding, Tom?" he asked.

Tom said that he had had a few lessons, but that Elizabeth was more interested than he was.

"Why don't we go out to your stable and have a little ride right now?" suggested Great Uncle Harry.

"That would be wonderful!" said Elizabeth.

"Can I come, too?" asked Tom.

"Of course," said Great Uncle Harry.

The creaky black taxi was called, and Great Uncle Harry, Elizabeth and Tom rode out to the edge of town to a stable with a sign that read "MISS HACKWORTH'S ENGLISH RIDING ACADEMY."

No one seemed to be around, but from inside the stable came the sound of a horse snorting, whinnying, stamping its feet and kicking the side of its stall.

"Sounds like an unhappy horse in there," observed Great Uncle Harry.

Miss Hackworth, a trim, middle-aged figure in jodhpurs, soon came out of the stable. She greeted Elizabeth in a friendly fashion, but was clearly upset with one of her horses.

"I can't get near Saladin today," she announced, to no one in particular. "He's impossible in the winter, when he doesn't get enough exercise."

"I have several horses like that out in Wyoming," said Great Uncle Harry. "I find that it's a question of getting their attention. May I have a little visit with Saladin?"

"Please do," said Miss Hackworth. "I'll put Elizabeth and Tom up on horses that they know."

Great Uncle Harry walked into the stable and approached the stall where a large black horse stood with his ears back, eyes rolled and nostrils flared. Great Uncle Harry rested his arms on the door to the stall and looked at the horse, who snorted nervously.

He spoke to the horse in low and steady tones. The horse's ears pricked up. After a few moments, the horse extended his nose and sniffed Great Uncle Harry's arm. Great Uncle Harry rubbed the horse's nose and then his ears. Continuing to talk, he entered the stall, carrying a bridle that hung on the gate. A few minutes later, he led a docile Saladin out of the stall and into the stable yard. Miss Hackworth was both pleased and amazed, and asked Great Uncle Harry if he would like to ride Saladin.

"I've never sat on one of those postage stamps," he said, referring to the English saddles he saw all around him.

"I have an old Western saddle inside," said Miss Hackworth. "I'll get it for you."

Great Uncle Harry quickly saddled Saladin with the Western saddle, while Miss Hackworth held the bridle. He took the reins and swung up into the saddle. Saladin pranced and snorted, but Great Uncle Harry kept him under control and walked him around the stable yard.

Miss Hackworth watched admiringly. "Saladin has met his equal in you," she said.

"He's a fine, spirited animal," said Great Uncle Harry, pleased with himself and with Saladin.

Elizabeth sat on her horse in a determined way, trying to remember all the things that Miss Hackworth had taught her during her summer lessons. Tom slouched in his saddle, less correct, but more at ease. Elizabeth led the way out of the stable yard to a dirt road that led invitingly away, between farm fields that lay empty and brown in the hazy winter sun. Great Uncle Harry brought up the rear and said, "You both look good in the saddle. But Elizabeth, you can relax a little more, and Tom you should hold the reins a little more firmly."

After they had walked for several minutes, Elizabeth said that she wanted to trot her horse. "Have at it," said Great Uncle Harry encouragingly.

Elizabeth pressed her horse, and it broke into a lumbering trot, breaking wind loudly and repeatedly as it did so. Elizabeth, humiliated, was blushing furiously.

Tom hooted with laughter. "Was that you, Elizabeth, or your horse?" he called out crudely.

Great Uncle Harry's shoulder shook with laughter. Elizabeth pulled her horse to a stop, and turned her angry face to her brother. "That's not nice, Tom, and you know it," Elizabeth lamented, her eyes brimming with embarrassed tears.

Great Uncle Harry cantered up beside her and patted her on the shoulder. "That happens to some horses in the winter when they don't get enough exercise," he said. "On the other hand," he added, "some horses do it all the time. On the way back in the taxi, I'll tell you about Jenny."

The rest of the ride was not a marked success from Elizabeth's point of view. She was anxious to show Great Uncle Harry how well she rode, but every time her horse went faster than a walk, the staccato gaseous explosions resumed. Tom would snicker, and Elizabeth even thought that she caught Great Uncle Harry laughing behind his hand. By the time they returned to the stable, Elizabeth was in a rage. She was angry with her horse, furious at Tom for laughing at her and disappointed that she had not been able to show Great Uncle Harry how well she could ride.

Miss Hackworth noted Elizabeth's unhappy expression as they entered the stable yard. "Elizabeth's horse farted the whole way," said Tom unhelpfully.

Great Uncle Harry quickly dismounted and hid his head behind Saladin's high shoulder, trying not to laugh.

"I'm sorry, Elizabeth," said Miss Hackworth. Turning to Tom she added severely, "You know that's not a nice word to use, Tom, particularly in mixed company."

"I NEVER want to ride that horse again!" wailed Elizabeth.

Great Uncle Harry had regained his composure and helped Elizabeth dismount. "Why don't you ride Saladin a few times around the ring?" Great Uncle Harry suggested.

"I'd love to," said Elizabeth. "Is that all right, Miss Hackworth?"

Miss Hackworth looked at Great Uncle Harry, who nodded. "I think that's fine," she said.

Great Uncle Harry lifted Elizabeth onto Saladin's back and adjusted the stirrups. "When you come out and visit me in Wyoming, this is the kind of saddle you'll ride. If Saladin gives you any trouble, just grab the saddle horn and hang on."

Big-eyed, Elizabeth nodded. It looked a long way down to the ground from Saladin's high back, but the thought of a visit to Wyoming was wildly exciting.

Still holding the reins, Great Uncle Harry looked into Saladin's left eye and spoke sternly. "Saladin, if you so much as twitch without Elizabeth's permission, I'm going to club you right between your mule ears. Is that clear?" As if in reply, Saladin snorted gently.

The big horse behaved perfectly as Elizabeth walked, trotted and then gently cantered around the ring. She never touched the saddle horn, but admitted to herself that it was very comforting to have it there. Elizabeth got off Saladin to expressions of praise and admiration from Great Uncle Harry and Miss Hackworth; even Tom said that she had "looked good". The afternoon had ultimately been a success, and they climbed in the old taxi to return in triumph to the Corliss home.

Chapter 9

Fartin' Jenny

On the way back home, Tom reminded Great Uncle Harry that he had promised to tell them about the horse named Jenny. Looking slightly uncomfortable, Great Uncle Harry turned to Elizabeth and asked if she would mind hearing a slightly vulgar story about a horse named "Fartin' Jenny". Elizabeth screwed up her face as though she were smelling something unpleasant.

"Come on, Great Uncle Harry, you promised," implored Tom.

Elizabeth turned and looked at her brother disdainfully and said, "You can tell the story just for

Tom." She put her fingers in her ears and shut her eyes tight.

"Well, Tom," said Great Uncle Harry, "when I was a boy in Ohio, my uncle had a farm a half mile outside of town. In the summer, I would help him cut hay, feed his stock, clean the barns, paint fences and that sort of thing. At the time, I had taken a shine to a pretty girl named Louisa, who lived on a farm about a mile away from my uncle's place. One hot Sunday afternoon, I had finished all my chores, so I asked my uncle if I could hitch up one of his horses to his buckboard and ride over to see Louisa. My uncle said that would be fine, but suggested that I take Jenny, who had not been out of the barn for some time." Great Uncle Harry paused and chuckled.

"My uncle had what you might call an 'earthy' sense of humor. He knew that I liked Louisa, and he also knew that Jenny had a tendency to fart. I guess he thought that the combination of Louisa, Jenny and me would be an interesting one. Well, I hitched up Jenny to the buckboard. She was a fat old bay with a big rump. I kept Jenny at a trot or a gallop all the way to Louisa's house, and was amazed at the amount of noise she made - it never stopped!" Great Uncle Harry turned to see if Elizabeth was listening.

Elizabeth *was* listening but pretended that she wasn't. When she saw Great Uncle Harry turn toward her, she stuck her fingers back into her ears and closed her eyes as tightly as she could. Great Uncle Harry smiled and continued his story.

"As Jenny and I came whirling into Louisa's driveway, I could see Louisa sitting on her front porch with another girl. I slowed Jenny to a walk, and we pulled up in front of the house in good order. Louisa seemed glad to see me, and invited me up onto the porch. Her friend's name was Helen, I believe. It was very hot on the porch, and after we sat there for a few minutes, Louisa suggested that we go for a ride, since it might be a little cooler along the road that ran beside the river."

"I got into the middle of the buckboard seat, with Louisa on one side of me and Helen on the other. It seemed to me that old Jenny's rump loomed in front of us like the backside of a barn. I walked Jenny out onto the road, and we turned toward the river. There were quite a few other people out for rides that day, and they passed us as we walked slowly along. The road was dry, and each passing wagon stirred up a cloud of dust, most of which seemed to land on us. Louisa brushed off her dress, and suggested that it might be cooler and less dusty if we moved a little faster. Fearing the worst, I shook the reins, and Jenny broke into a trot." Great Uncle Harry's shoulders shook with silent laughter.

"Well, as soon as Jenny started to trot she began to fart. I felt my face turning red, and both girls put their hands to their faces and turned away from me. I knew that they were both laughing. They were farm girls and knew about animals, but in those days you couldn't admit that something like that was funny.

On we went, and I tried to think of something to say. Finally, out of desperation I said, 'I hear thunder; I wonder if it will rain?' That wasn't very clever of me, but it gave us all an excuse to laugh. I thought Louisa was going to fall off the buckboard, she was laughing so hard! When we got to the river, I pulled off the road, and we sat in the grass and talked and laughed all afternoon. I never had such a good time with Louisa. Maybe old Jenny did us a favor and broke the ice."

"That's a nice story," said Elizabeth, no longer pretending not to listen.

"Yes, I think it is, too," said Great Uncle Harry. "The last person I told that story to was your Grandma Mary, but she didn't like it as much as you did."

The taxi pulled up to the Corliss house, and Elizabeth ran ahead to tell her mother about her ride and the possibility of a visit to Wyoming.

Chapter 10

A Visit to the Crows

Elizabeth sat at the foot of the stairs, waiting for Great Uncle Harry to come down from an afternoon nap. She was full of questions, and was worried that Great Uncle Harry's visit would end before she was able to learn more about Sam Pickett, her grandmother and the double eagle. After what seemed a very long time, Elizabeth heard her great uncle open the door to his room. She waited for him at the foot of the stairs.

"I have a lot of questions to ask you," she said.

"I hope I'm able to answer them," said Great Uncle Harry, with a smile.

In the living room, Elizabeth sat on a footstool, facing Great Uncle Harry. "I don't know which questions to ask first," she said. She saw that Great Uncle Harry was idly rubbing the double eagle with the tips of his fingers, so she started her questions with the coin.

"How did Sam get the double eagle back?" asked Elizabeth.

"I'll be glad to tell you that story," said Great Uncle Harry, lighting his pipe and settling back in his chair. "Sam rested up after his long run, and afterward decided that he would go back into Crow country and find out once and for all whether he could trap in their territory without running the risk of getting scalped. He pulled together some horses, mules, food and guns, and then, out of the blue, asked me to go with him. I was happy to accept."

Sam Pickett and Harry Renick lay on their stomachs at the top of the ridge, looking down at a big Crow encampment. Sam was peering through a telescope, and was pleased with what he saw. "Broken Lance's people are down there, and so are the Crows that caught me." Sam handed Harry the telescope. "You can see that the lodges are pitched in two semi-circles. Broken Lance's branch of the tribe is on the left, and the Big Nose bunch is on the right."

"You got a plan?" asked Harry hopefully.

Sam scratched his beard. "I guess we'll ride right up to Broken Lance's lodge and pay him a call. I have some presents for him, and after some palaver we'll get around to discussing what happened to me. Broken Lance will know all about it already."

Sam and Harry crawled back to their horses, mounted and rode to the top of the ridge overlooking the Indian camp. There they stood for several minutes, until it was clear that they had been seen and identified. Then they rode slowly down into the village and approached the largest lodge, which stood in the middle of the semicircle. Harry had never been in an Indian village, and was impressed by the brightly painted lodges. Indians were gathered at the lodge entrances, and looked at Sam and Harry with impassive faces. A tall Indian stood, arms folded, outside the central tent. Sam pulled his horse to a stop, raised his right hand in greeting, and spoke in the Crow tongue. The tall Indian answered, and also raised his hand in greeting. Sam turned to Harry and spoke again. The Indian smiled, and gestured for them to dismount. "I told Broken Lance that I brought you along because your left arm is stronger than mine. He said he'd be careful not to make you angry."

Sam dismounted, and took from one of his pack mules a package wrapped in canvas. "Gifts," he said. Sam and Harry followed Broken Lance to a grove of trees behind his lodge. They sat in a circle in the shade, near a river that ran past the camp. Several other Indians joined them.

Sam unrolled the canvas wrapping, and passed around gifts of cloth, beads and tobacco. To Broken Lance he gave a new hunting knife. The Indians received their gifts with dignity and appreciation. A conversation followed, between Sam and Broken Lance. Sam used sign language as well as the Crow tongue, so Harry was able to understand at least part of what was being discussed. A long pipe was lighted, and passed around to each of the men sitting in the shade. Harry felt quite at ease, and was impressed by the dignified Indians who listened to Sam and Broken Lance with both interest and respect.

As the talk continued, small children quietly approached and sat in the background, listening to the words of their elders. At dusk, a handsome woman walked into the circle and spoke to Broken Lance. Sam rose and smiled at her. Harry also got up. "This is Blue Dawn, the wife of Broken Lance," said Sam. "She sort of adopted me the winter that I got stuck in the mountains. She has invited us to join them for the evening meal."

As they walked to Broken Lance's lodge, Sam reported that the conversation had gone well, that they both were welcome in Broken Lance's village, and that the problem with Big Nose would be talked about later. They ate in the warmth of Broken Lance's lodge. Blue Dawn made Harry feel at home with pats on his shoulder, smiles and tender bits of venison that she personally cooked for him.

A wind from the west blew through the Crow camp, bringing with it a coolness from the mountaintops. The lodge poles creaked, and smoke from the fire swirled through the tent. Broken Lance rose and went outside. "He's going to fix the flaps around the smoke hole so that the fire will draw better," explained Sam. Harry looked up to the hole at the top of the conical tent and saw that the smoke was once again rising straight from the fire. Broken Lance returned and sat on his buffalo robe. Blue Dawn pointed to the walls of the lodge and spoke. Sam translated, "She says that this tent is made of the skins of twenty-four buffalo. She tanned and scraped the skins herself, and sewed them together with the help of her mother. She says it is the best lodge in the village. It does not leak, and it will not blow down. This is her home, she is very proud of it and she is glad to share it with us."

Having made this speech, Blue Dawn lay down with her back to the fire, and pulled a robe over her head and shoulders. The wind blew harder, the lodge poles bent and the skins shifted and moved gently like sails on a vessel. Harry felt a sense of peace and harmony that he had never felt before.

From the shadows across the lodge came the deep voice of Broken Lance, who was lying on his side with his head propped on his hand. Harry's eyes drooped, he lay down and was quickly asleep. Sam and Broken Lance talked deep into the night.

Chapter 11

The Sign of Broken Lance

The next morning, Harry woke up to find that he was alone in the lodge. He stuck his head outside, and found that the wind had died and the sky was clear. He went down to the river. Along its banks, Crow children were playing. They gathered around Harry as he washed his face. He had brought his razor and a small mirror with him, and the Indian children watched, open-mouthed, as he lathered his face, sharpened his razor on his buckskin pant leg, and then began to shave. The giggling and pointing of fingers continued throughout. When he had finished this strange process that the Indian children did not understand, Harry handed the mirror to a pretty little girl so that she could admire herself. The children passed the mirror around until each one had had a chance to look.

Sam approached quietly and was squatting on his heels on the bank above the edge of the stream. "If you grew a beard like me, Lefty, you wouldn't have to go through that damnable process," Sam remarked. Harry joined him at the top of the bank.

"We're in good shape," said Sam in a confident tone. "Broken Lance knew all about my run-in with Big Nose, and told me I had done about the best I could under the circumstances. Big Nose's real name is Crazy Bear, and he is war chief of that other band of Crows. He has a hot temper and wants to fight the white man. Broken Lance said that maybe my only mistake was not to kill Crazy Bear when I had the chance. He was glad I had not killed any of the other Indians who were chasing me, particularly No Feathers, who is the son of the chief of that other village. One Buck's shoulder wound is healing, and he told the village how brave No Feathers was when he counted coup on me. As a result of that, No Feathers has a new name, and can wear an eagle feather in his hair."

"What's his new name?" asked Harry.

"He's called 'Runs Not Afraid'," said Sam. He made a wry face. "They'll always be Big Nose and No Feathers, as far as I'm concerned," he said.

"Our only problem is Big Nose. He hates my guts,

and Broken Lance says that he'll try to kill me the first chance he gets. I don't think he can bring the rest of the braves from his village along with him, so we just have this one wild man to worry about. Anyway, it's not enough to give me the fantods. I'll come back and trap some, but I'll stay more or less in Broken Lance's area, and keep away from Big Nose."

Sam and Harry walked back toward Broken Lance's lodge. Sam stopped. "By God, there are the horses and mules that Big Nose stole from me." They saw Broken Lance talking with two other braves outside his lodge. "That's No Feathers and One Buck," said Sam out of the side of his mouth. "I'll be interested to see how they react to me."

The three Indians watched Sam and Harry approach. Harry thought that their expressions were friendly. Sam gave the greeting sign and walked up to One Buck, who had his right arm tied in a rudimentary sling. Sam gently touched One Buck's shoulder, and spoke to him. One Buck replied, touched his shoulder and nodded positively. Sam then turned to No Feathers, and pointed admiringly to the long eagle feather pinned in the young brave's hair. No Feathers smiled, touched his heart with his hand, and then reached out and touched Sam's heart. Sam then went to each of the horses and mules, touched them, and then turned and faced Broken Lance. He spoke at some length, and then gestured at the animals in a way that made it clear that he was giving them all back to the three Indians in front of him. No Feathers put his hand to his mouth in amazement. Sam again spoke out of the side of his mouth to Harry. "I think of these animals as a kind of rent I'm paying so I can come back to these parts safely in the future."

Broken Lance invited Sam and Harry into his lodge, where Blue Dawn waited. She served them a delicious meat stew in carved wooden plates that they ate with their fingers.

After the meal, Broken Lance lifted a buffalo robe which had lain beside him. Under it were the guns and traps from Sam's previous expedition. Sam accepted them with thanks. Broken Lance then took something from a deerskin pouch and handed it to Sam. It was the double eagle with a new buckskin thong. Sam looked at it and passed it to Harry. He spoke words of thanks to Broken Lance. Then Blue Dawn spoke, and Broken Lance turned to try to hush her. Sam said, "Blue Dawn just told me that Broken Lance had to trade one of his best horses to Big Nose to get the double eagle back. She thanked me for giving Broken Lance a good horse outside the lodge. I think this is all working out just fine."

Broken Lance spoke, pointing to the double eagle in Harry's hand. "He said that he cut his sign into the face of the coin, and that anyone carrying the coin will be safe in his territory." Harry looked at the double eagle, and saw that a broken lance had been cut across its face. He handed the coin to Sam, who proudly put it back around his own neck.

Sam and Harry then packed up and got ready to head back to the trading post. All of the villagers gathered around as they prepared to leave. Harry saw the little girl who had watched him shave and tossed her his mirror. She laughed and pressed the mirror to her chest. Harry's heart was full, and he wished that he could speak to the Crow in their language.

At the top of the ridge above the village, Sam and Harry paused and looked back. They waved, and the Indians waved back. They turned and vanished over the horizon.

Chief Broken Lance

Chapter 12

Mary Atherton Arrives Out West

"What about Grandma?" Elizabeth asked.

Great Uncle Harry looked out the window and rubbed his hand across his face. "Well, the trading post where I worked got bigger as the years passed. We worked mostly with the peaceful Crow Indians, so more and more people came and built houses around the original trading post, which had been a kind of fort. Families started coming in, and soon we had ten or twelve children running around, more or less wild. The families got together and decided that they needed a schoolteacher. The owners of the trading post were in favor of this because they knew that the more people came, the more business they would have. So they offered to build a two-room school, right alongside the stockade walls, where it would be safe. One room would be for the teacher, and the other would be for the classroom. One of the women knew of a school back east that trained young people to be teachers, so she wrote a letter to the school, asking that one of its graduates consider coming out West to 'bring education and enlightenment to the heathen'."

Elizabeth giggled.

"The result of this was that Mary Atherton, your grandma, agreed to come. We got a letter saying that she would be arriving on the steamboat that came up the river every month or so. Most of the people from the trading post rode over to the landing to meet your grandma, as her arrival was seen as a great step toward civilizing our area, which was certainly needed."

"Sam Pickett was hanging around the trading post the day your grandma arrived, and I asked him if he intended to be part of the greeting party at the landing. He snorted and said that he was too old to be educated, but I noticed him up on the bluff overlooking the river when the steamboat came in."

Great Uncle Harry raised his head and looked at the ceiling. "I can still see your grandma, standing on the upper deck of the steamboat, looking at us and at the big empty country that lay all around, as far as the eye could see. We all waved at her and she waved back. I heard a horse gallop up behind me. It was Sam. He watched your grandma walk off the steamboat and his eyes were blazing, as though some beautiful, unknown bird had suddenly flown into his life. Sam fell in love with your grandma the first moment he laid eyes on her." Great Uncle Harry paused and sighed.

"What about you, Great Uncle Harry?" asked Elizabeth.

"What do you mean, what about me?" he said.

"I mean, how did you feel about Grandma when you first saw her?" said Elizabeth.

"I thought that she was the most beautiful woman I ever saw, and I still do," said Great Uncle Harry. His eyes were sad.

"Then what happened?" asked Elizabeth.

"Well, your grandma settled right in and started teaching school two days after she arrived. She became the center of life for all of us, because she brought with her a beauty and gentleness that hadn't been here before she came."

"Sam, as I say, lost his heart to her completely, and he began to follow her around like a great lost puppy. He would do anything for her, and your grandma used Sam to get a lot of improvements made in the schoolhouse."

"How did Grandma like Sam?" asked Elizabeth.

"I think she was a little afraid of him. She'd never seen anybody like Sam before, and Sam, who had never had anything to do with a refined lady, didn't know what to say to her or how to act. Your grandma was always gentle with Sam. She saw his great strengths, and she admired a lot of things about him."

"What kind of things did she like about Sam?" asked Elizabeth.

"Well your grandma saw that he had real respect and admiration for the Indians. Most of the people out West in those days treated Indians like dangerous animals, but Sam knew them, liked them and understood them. One time, your grandma heard that Broken Lance's village was just a few miles away from the trading post. She asked Sam and me to take her for a visit. We were glad to oblige, so the three of us rode out one bright Sunday morning. Broken Lance and Blue Dawn greeted us as friends and made your grandma feel welcome. They had had a daughter by that time - she was about your age. She had long black braids and big eyes, and was always asking questions. I guess all little girls do that, don't they Elizabeth?" asked Great Uncle Harry with a smile.

"Mother says that if we don't ask questions, we won't learn about things," said Elizabeth. "Then what happened?"

"Well your grandma became interested in Blue Dawn's daughter. She knew from Sam that the Crow were about the only tribe to be helpful to the white settlers, because their chiefs were wise enough to see that the white man was coming, and that it was no use to fight him. The other tribes - the Sioux, Cheyenne and Blackfeet - never learned that, and their people suffered. And today, the Crow still live on their land, or at least a good part of it, while the other tribes have vanished into Canada, or are living in land on reservations that no one wants. Your grandma knew that the Crow were peaceful and wanted to live peacefully with white people, so she had the thought that some Crow children ought to learn to speak English. No one had ever thought of that before, but right there, in Broken Lance's village, your grandma offered to teach Blue Dawn's daughter as a student in her school. Broken Lance and Blue Dawn were amazed by this offer, and didn't know what to say. They knew that your grandma was offering something that she thought was good, and they appreciated that. But they didn't want to have their daughter move away and live a new and strange life among white people. It was an awkward moment."

"Sam said something to Broken Lance in the Crow tongue, and then told your grandma that her offer was appreciated, but that they would need some time to think it over. Your grandma understood that, and the moment passed."

"Just then we heard some yelling and whooping outside Broken Lance's lodge. It was a Crow war party returning from a raid on a Blackfeet village. They had stolen horses and taken three Blackfeet scalps; the entire Crow village was overjoyed. The war party rode their horses around the lodges, waving the scalps and showing off the stolen horses. It was a good moment for the Crows, but your grandma was horrified. I thought she was going to faint."

"We quickly rode out of the village, and on the way back, she kept saying that she could not understand how wonderful people like Broken Lance and Blue Dawn could approve of such terrible things as taking scalps and stealing horses. We tried to explain, but your grandma couldn't understand." Great Uncle Harry paused. "I guess it was from that moment that I knew your grandma would not stay out West. She was too gentle, and the wildness of the place frightened her."

"Is that why she didn't marry you or Sam?" asked Elizabeth.

Mrs. Corliss stood in the doorway and looked at Great Uncle Harry the way she had looked at a sparrow with a broken wing that Tom brought home one evening. Turning to Elizabeth, Mrs. Corliss said, "Elizabeth, please help me set the table for supper. You have asked Great Uncle Harry enough questions for today."

Great Uncle Harry scratched his nose. "Some other things happened to your grandma that made it clear that she wouldn't be happy there, so she married my brother Frank, who could give her the kind of life she wanted." Great Uncle Harry saw that Elizabeth was looking sad, so he went over to her and hugged her. "If your grandma hadn't married Frank, your mother wouldn't have been born, and you and I wouldn't be here talking today. So, it ended all right," said Great Uncle Harry firmly.

"That's true," said Elizabeth. "But still..." Her voice trailed off.

Great Uncle Harry released Elizabeth and said, "Go help your mother with supper." With a sigh, Elizabeth headed for the kitchen.

Chapter 13

Aces Beat Kings

After the supper dishes had been cleared away, Great Uncle Harry remained at the table. Reaching into his pocket, he produced a pack of playing cards and shuffled them, over and over. Then he carefully began to lay out the cards in a complicated pattern. Elizabeth and Tom came out of the kitchen and watched him. Great Uncle Harry's large hands moved smoothly as he dealt the cards.

"What are you playing?" asked Elizabeth.

"It's a game of solitaire called Idiot's Delight," replied Great Uncle Harry. "It's a good way to spend time when you're snowed in in Wyoming."

"Do you know how to play Go Fish?" asked Elizabeth, naming the only card game she knew.

"No, I don't," said Great Uncle Harry, "but I do know how to play Hearts."

"How do you play it?" asked Tom and Elizabeth in unison.

Great Uncle Harry explained the game, and Tom and Elizabeth quickly got the main points, which were to avoid taking any hearts, and above all to avoid taking the queen of spades, which Great Uncle Harry referred to as "Dirty Sal". Great Uncle Harry dealt a hand, but Elizabeth couldn't hold so many cards and kept dropping them. Tom grew annoyed and said, "Come on Elizabeth, hold onto your cards."

"I can't," said Elizabeth, "there are too many of them."

Great Uncle Harry said gently, "Why don't you ask your Mother to play? It's a better game with four players, and you won't have so many cards to hold."

Mrs. Corliss came out of the kitchen, and play commenced. Tom proved to have good card sense, and held strong hands of cards. He succeeded in giving Elizabeth the queen of spades three times in a row. The game ended with Elizabeth losing by a wide margin. Tom teased her as she went off to bed. Elizabeth couldn't think of anything clever to say in return, so she departed with a very sorrowful expression on her face, even though her mother had given her a hug and whispered into her ear.

Great Uncle Harry watched all of this silently. He continued to sit at the table and dealt himself another game of "Idiot's Delight". Tom was feeling very pleased with himself and watched Great Uncle Harry play. After a few minutes Tom asked him, "Do you know how to play poker?"

"I've played a few hands along the way," said Great Uncle Harry, looking into Tom's eyes.

"Let's play some hands," suggested Tom.

Great Uncle Harry looked hard at Tom and, narrowing his eyes, said, "Poker is only a game to be played for money."

This slowed Tom down a little, and then he thought of the large jar full of pennies that he had in his room. "I've got money," he said. "Let's play."

Tom ran up to his room and returned with the penny jar. "Sell me a hundred," said Great Uncle Harry, taking a silver dollar out of his pocket. The sight of the silver dollar frightened Tom a little bit, and he sensed that he might be getting into deep water. "Great Uncle Harry, will you please write down the way the hands rank? Sometimes I get mixed up," said Tom.

Harry pulled an envelope out of his coat, and in neat lettering, wrote out the ranking of the hands:

1 Pair
2 Pair
3 of a Kind
Straight

Flush
Full House
4 of a Kind
Straight Flush

Tom studied the list carefully. "What's the difference between a straight and a flush?" he asked, half embarrassed.

"A straight is five cards in sequence, not of the same suit, and a flush is five cards of the same suit, not in sequence," replied Great Uncle Harry. "You sure you want to play, Tom?" asked Harry, smiling to himself.

Tom gulped, but said, "Oh yes, I really want to."

They cut the cards for deal and Great Uncle Harry won, cutting a jack to Tom's three.

"I only know how to play draw and five card stud," said Tom, nervously.

"Those are the best games," said Great Uncle Harry evenly. "We'll start with a game of draw."

Tom had a pair of queens, but lost to Great Uncle Harry's three sevens. That seemed to set the pattern of play, for Tom lost practically every hand. After thirty minutes, Tom's penny jar was almost empty, while Great Uncle Harry had won his silver dollar back and had a large pile of pennies in front of him. Tom's heart was beating very fast, and he felt almost powerless.

Great Uncle Harry shuffled the cards several times and said, "You're almost cleaned out, Tom, shall we make this the last hand?"

"I guess we'd better," said Tom in a small voice.

"Let's make it draw," said Great Uncle Harry, as the cards flicked smoothly under his long fingers. Tom picked up his five cards and could not believe his eyes - he held four kings. He quickly looked at the list. His hands began to sweat and he felt his eyes water. Trying desperately to act casual, Tom pretended to yawn and stared at his cards at great length. "I guess I'll take one card," he said, trying to sound discouraged.

" Aren't you going to bet first?" asked Great Uncle Harry.

"Oh yes!" said Tom. He counted out the few pennies in his jar. There were twelve. "I'll bet these," said Tom.

"I'll call that bet, and raise you a dollar," said Great Uncle Harry in an implacable tone.

"I don't have any more money, Great Uncle Harry," said Tom helplessly.

"Yes you do. You have those silver dollars I gave you for Christmas," said Great Uncle Harry.

Tom's heart leaped. "Oh yes, I'd forgotten. I'll get them." He ran upstairs and got the silver dollars from his bureau. He rushed back to the dining room table and pushed one dollar forward to match Great Uncle Harry's bet. "I'll still take one card," he said.

"I'll take three," said Great Uncle Harry placidly. "It's your bet, Tom."

Tom had hardly looked at the card he had drawn, knowing that he had the four kings. "I'll bet my last two dollars," said Tom.

Great Uncle Harry stared hard at Tom, and said "I'll call you. Let's see what you have."

"I've got four kings," said Tom proudly.

Great Uncle Harry put down his hand and turned the cards over, one by one. Tom watched in growing horror as Great Uncle Harry turned over the first three cards. They were all aces. The fourth card was a six. Great Uncle Harry paused for a moment and then turned over the final card. It was the fourth ace. Tom slumped in his chair. His eyes smarted, his heart beat wildly and he had to fight to keep from crying. Great Uncle Harry calmly pulled the pennies and the silver dollars in front of him. He put the dollars in his pocket and the pennies in the jar without speaking.

"Bad luck, Tom," he said finally.

Tom got up from his chair, wiped his eyes and said unsteadily, "Good night, Great Uncle Harry. Thank you for the game." He turned and stumbled out of the room. Great Uncle Harry watched him go, and slowly a smile spread over his face. He picked up the cards and walked into the living room.

Chapter 14

Great Uncle Harry's Plans

Mrs. Corliss came downstairs from checking on both of her children, and found Great Uncle Harry smoking in front of the fire. "I don't know how I feel about card playing after tonight. Elizabeth is furious at Tom for making her lose at Hearts, and Tom feels miserable about losing his silver dollars. The pennies didn't matter so much, but those silver dollars...you were really hard on him, Uncle Harry," she said reproachfully.

"Yes, I was," Great Uncle Harry said, looking a little guilty. "I tried to teach him two lessons at once, and maybe I shouldn't have done that."

"What were the lessons?" asked Mrs. Corliss.

"Well, I was angry at Tom for giving Elizabeth 'Dirty Sal' three times in a row, and I wanted him to feel what it's like to lose. Then, once we got into the game, I decided to show Tom how dangerous it can be to play poker with people you don't know. I guess I didn't need to make the lesson so painful."

"Tom said that you held four aces in the last hand. Did you do that purposely, Uncle Harry?"

"Yes, and I dealt him four kings so he'd bet all his money," said Great Uncle Harry, looking uncomfortable. "I really admired the way Tom handled it. He took it like a man and thanked me for the game. That boy's going to be all right." Great Uncle Harry paused and looked at Mrs. Corliss. "You know how I feel about Elizabeth, don't you?" he asked softly.

"Yes, I do," said Mrs. Corliss, patting Great Uncle Harry's hand. "And she feels the same way about you." There was a period of silence, then Mr. Corliss walked into the living room.

Great Uncle Harry spoke to both of them, "I think it's about time that I headed back to the ranch. I don't want to wear out my welcome."

"You couldn't do that, no matter how long you stayed," said Mrs. Corliss. "Why don't you stay with us until spring?"

"I couldn't do that," said Great Uncle Harry. "The ranch hands would run wild, the bears would break into the kitchen and the mules would start consorting with the cow ponies!"

Mr. Corliss laughed. "Uncle Harry, you have made a deep and wonderful impression on our two children. They'll never forget you."

Great Uncle Harry smiled. "I love them both. Makes me realize how much I miss not having a family of my own. But, I think it's better that I go."

"Why?" said Mrs. Corliss.

"You sound just like Elizabeth when you ask me that," said Great Uncle Harry.

"Elizabeth's the reason I should go. She has a mind like a freight train coming down the track. She's bound and determined to find out all about her Grandma out West, and there are some parts of that story that she's not ready to hear."

Mrs. Corliss sighed and glanced at her husband. He looked at Great Uncle Harry and said, "You mean the parts about when Elizabeth's grandma was taken away by the Indians?"

"Yes, I mean that, and what happened afterward with Big Nose and Broken Lance. That's pretty rough. I'd rather Elizabeth hear about that when she's older." He paused. "I tell you what. I've mentioned to Tom and Elizabeth about coming out to Wyoming, and they seemed to like the idea. Why don't you give me three or four summers to make the ranch more civilized, and by then Tom and Elizabeth will be old enough to come out and visit me by themselves."

"That sounds wonderful, Uncle Harry," said Mrs. Corliss, "but three or four years is a long time." She paused, embarrassed by what she had said.

Great Uncle Harry laughed. "Don't worry about me, I'm going to live forever."

Chapter 15

Lessons from Losses

It had taken Tom a long time to get to sleep the night before. He kept thinking about the silver dollars, and how much he had liked having them. He also kept wondering about Great Uncle Harry, for in the poker game he had seen a hard side to the old man that had he had not seen before. Tom felt that he had been given a look at things that he was not yet ready to handle. He went down to breakfast feeling very vulnerable, as though something had been taken from him that he could not quite identify.

Mrs. Corliss was in the kitchen at breakfast, talking to Elizabeth. They both looked at Tom. Elizabeth frowned and said, "I hear that Great Uncle Harry took all your money at poker last night." Elizabeth clapped her hand to her mouth and giggled.

"It's nothing to laugh about," said Tom, angrily. "I feel terrible about losing those silver dollars. I'm going to see if I can earn them back from Great Uncle Harry by shining his boots or something."

Mrs. Corliss served Tom some hot oatmeal and told him to take it into the dining room, where his place was set. Tom entered the dining room and immediately saw his jar of pennies sitting on the table by his napkin. He rushed to the table, and saw that inside the jar were his three silver dollars. Under the jar was a small piece of paper, folded in half. Tom snatched up the paper and unfolded it. On it, in Great Uncle Harry's neat handwriting, two sentences were written:

Know who you are playing with.

Only bet what you don't mind losing.

Tom was pondering those bits of wisdom when he heard the front door open. It was Great Uncle Harry, returning from an early morning walk. Tom went to the door, and looking up at his tall great uncle he said, "Thank you, Great Uncle Harry. That was a hard lesson you taught me, and I truly appreciate your returning my money to me."

Great Uncle Harry put out his hand. "Tom, I really admired you last night. We all lose some things along the way, but the important thing is to keep your dignity, win or lose." They shook hands, and Tom felt that whatever had been taken away from him had been restored. He went back to the dining room, and ate three helpings of oatmeal with a happy heart.

Chapter 16

Dreams of Wyoming

That night at supper, Great Uncle Harry announced that he would return to Wyoming the next day. Elizabeth and Tom were shocked, and both began to protest loudly, urging Great Uncle Harry to stay. Elizabeth got up from her chair, went around to Great Uncle Harry and put her arms around him. "Don't go, Great Uncle Harry, please don't go," she pleaded.

Great Uncle Harry rubbed his eyes and looked very sad. Suddenly he brightened, and picked Elizabeth up and placed her in his lap. Looking at her seriously he said, "I'll tell you what, Elizabeth, my favorite mare is going to foal pretty soon, and I want to be there. If the foal is a good one, I'll train it especially for you, so that when you and Tom come to visit me, you'll have your own special horse." Great Uncle Harry looked over the top of Elizabeth's head at Tom and said, "I already have a pinto in mind for you, Tom."

Elizabeth was still sad about Great Uncle Harry's leaving, but the prospect of a visit to Wyoming, and a horse just for her eased her sadness. As she prepared to go to bed, Elizabeth asked Great Uncle Harry if he would come up and tuck her in. He said he'd be glad to.

A little later, Great Uncle Harry climbed the stairs to Elizabeth's room. She was waiting for him. "When will I go out to Wyoming to see you?" asked Elizabeth.

Great Uncle Harry answered, somewhat evasively, "It will take me a while to make the old place presentable for you and Tom. And we want the young horse to be ready for you to ride."

"So it won't be this year, will it?" said Elizabeth sadly.

"No, I guess not," said Great Uncle Harry. Sensing Elizabeth's sadness, Great Uncle Harry began to sing softly to her, in words that she did not understand. Great Uncle Harry had a deep voice, and Elizabeth closed her eyes as she listened. "I like that, Great Uncle Harry. Is it a lullaby?" asked Elizabeth.

"It's a Crow song that I heard Blue Dawn sing to her daughter to get her to go to sleep," replied Great Uncle Harry.

"What do the words mean?" asked Elizabeth.

"Oh, it's hard to translate, but it means something like this," said Great Uncle Harry, who then sang the words in English:

Oh, close your eyes and go to sleep.
The light is fading in the west,
Clouds drift across the moon,
And all the village is at rest.

Great Uncle Harry held Elizabeth's hand and sang the song over and over, in the Crow tongue. He felt her hand relax, and her deep breathing told him that she was asleep. Great Uncle Harry rose and looked at Elizabeth in the half-light. He bent and kissed her forehead, turned and slowly left the room. In the morning he was gone.

Chapter 17

What's a 'Dear Man'?

January 22, 1922

Dear Grandma,

How are you? I am fine. Thank you for your lovely Christmas present. I like it very much.

Great Uncle Harry was here for Christmas. He went back to Wyoming a few days ago. He told us lots about you and Sam Pickett and the old days, but he left before he told me everything I want to know. Why didn't you stay out West? Why didn't you marry Sam Pickett? What about Great Uncle Harry? Are you happy?

Happy New Year!
Love,
Elizabeth

* * * * * *

March 15, 1922

My Dear Elizabeth,

I'm sorry that it has taken me so long to answer your letter. Things here have been hectic, and time seems to slip away so fast.

I was glad to hear that Harry was with you for the holidays. He is a dear man, and so was Sam Pickett, in his way. Those days were long ago, and I guess that Harry thinks about them more than I do.

I have been very happy here in Boston. Your Grandfather Frank is a wonderful provider, and I believe that I was not meant to live out on the edge of things, as exciting as that might have been. There was a savage side to life out there that I could not abide. So, I believe that it was meant to be that I would meet Frank, and that he would bring me back here to a life that I have enjoyed.

Yes, I am happy.
Much love,
Your Grandmother Mary

* * * * * *

Elizabeth walked into the kitchen holding her grandmother's letter. Mrs. Corliss was peeling potatoes for supper, and Elizabeth sat at the kitchen table, frowning slightly, with her chin in her hand.

"I don't really like this letter from Grandma," said Elizabeth.

"Why is that?" asked her mother.

Elizabeth sighed. "I guess it's because she didn't answer my questions and, besides, she didn't answer for a long time."

"I think she did answer your questions, at least indirectly," said Mrs. Corliss.

"What does it mean when Grandma calls Great Uncle Harry 'a dear man'?" Elizabeth asked.

Mrs. Corliss stopped peeling potatoes and looked away. "That's a very grown-up question, Elizabeth," she said gently. "I would say that when a woman calls someone a 'dear man', it means that at one time he meant something to her that he doesn't mean anymore."

Elizabeth's face crumpled. "I don't like that, I don't like that at all. Great Uncle Harry's wonderful. That really makes me sad."

Mrs. Corliss went to Elizabeth and hugged her. "Don't take on the whole world," she said softly.

"I'm not," Elizabeth sniffed. "But still..."

Chapter 18

Impatience on the Platform

April 23, 1923

Elizabeth stood beside her father on the railway station platform, waiting for the train that would bring her grandparents for a visit. Grandmother Mary and Grandfather Frank were on their way back to Boston from a winter in Florida. Elizabeth had not seen either of them for three years, so she waited impatiently for the train to appear. Steam engines fascinated Elizabeth. They were so massive, yet moved so smoothly, and the sound of their haunting whistles, especially at night, always set Elizabeth thinking about the distant places that she hoped one day to see.

Two short hoots made Elizabeth jump, and she leaned forward to look down the tracks. Around a distant bend, the great black engine appeared. Gray smoke poured out of the smokestack, and white puffs of steam spilled from its front wheels. Elizabeth ran to the end of the platform to meet the train. The engineer, wearing a blue hat with a long bill, smiled down at her and waved. White steam swirled around her as the engine passed, its giant piston arms moving with slow precision.

With a final burst of steam, the train stopped. Elizabeth ran back up the platform, looking into the windows of the Pullman cars, hoping to see a face that she knew. Porters in white coats swung down to the platform, carrying metal stools they placed at the foot of the railcar steps. The porters then went back onto the train and appeared again, carrying the luggage of their passengers. At last, next to a large array of baggage, Elizabeth saw the familiar figure of her grandfather. He stepped carefully down onto the stool, then turned to help his wife descend. Elizabeth ran toward them, thinking that Grandfather Frank had grown heavier since she had seen him last, and that he was not as tall as Great Uncle Harry.

Mary Renick seemed unchanged. Wearing a stylish hat and a dark coat with a gray fur collar, her step was youthful and her smile brilliant. Elizabeth rushed into her arms and hugged her as hard as she could. Grandmother Mary even smelled wonderful, wearing a fragrance totally new to Elizabeth.

Grandmother Mary held Elizabeth at arm's length to get a good look at her, and their eyes searched each other's faces. "Elizabeth, you're a beautiful young girl," said Grandmother Mary.

Elizabeth lowered her head, blushing. She wished that her eyes were green like her grandmother's instead of brown. She turned to greet her grandfather, who stood, hat in hand, waiting to be recognized. Elizabeth hugged her grandfather. His face reminded her of Great Uncle Harry, but there was no mustache, and the face she saw in front of her now was round and soft, while the face she remembered had been square and hard.

"Well, young lady, you are looking more and more like your mother," said Grandfather Frank. Elizabeth smiled and was glad that her grandparents had come to visit.

Thirty minutes later, a two-car procession arrived at the Corliss home. There had been too much Renick baggage to fit into the family's Ford Model T, so the creaky black taxi had been hired to bring the trunks and suitcases. Elizabeth wondered what in the world could be in all of those pieces of luggage, but she hid her curiosity and said nothing.

Mrs. Corliss and Tom were waiting on the porch as they drove up. Elizabeth watched as her mother and her grandmother embraced. They were very much alike - both graceful and almost like sisters, rather than mother and daughter. As she watched, Elizabeth was full of love for both of them, but she had questions for her grandmother.

Chapter 19

Questions for Grandmother Mary

Mary Renick was brushing her hair. It was long and heavy, still more dark red than gray. When she turned her head gracefully so that the brush could reach the ends of her hair, she saw Elizabeth standing in the door, looking at her intently. "Come in, Elizabeth, it's so good to be with you all again. I can't believe how you and Tom have grown."

Elizabeth came in, sat on the edge of the bed and watched as her grandmother quickly pinned up her hair. "You have lovely, long hair, Elizabeth," said her grandmother. "I wish my hair was still the color of yours." Elizabeth smiled but said nothing.

Mary Renick turned to look at her granddaughter directly. "Elizabeth, there is something on your mind; tell me what it is."

Elizabeth looked away. "I want to know about when you were out West, and why..." Her voice trailed off.

"Why - what a hard question to deal with," Mary said as she sat beside Elizabeth on the bed and hugged her. She saw that Elizabeth had something in her hands. "What are you holding, Elizabeth?" she asked.

"These are the silver dollars that Great Uncle Harry gave me. I wanted to show them to you." Elizabeth spread the three coins out on the bed. "At first I wanted all new, shiny ones, but then Great Uncle Harry explained about how the dates meant so much, and how old coins had been a part of so many people's lives. I love them; I'll never spend them."

Mary reached out and touched each coin with the tip of her long and slender finger. "They are lovely. Silver ages so well, better than most people." She sighed. "Yes, looking at these coins does take me back." As though a door had opened in her mind, Mary said, "What can I tell you about those days, Elizabeth? They were long ago, but I remember them well."

Elizabeth scratched her nose. "Well, how did you feel when you went up that big river and arrived at the place where you were going to teach school?"

Mary got up from the bed and went to the window. She spoke without turning. "I thought that I had never seen such an empty and desolate place. The river was muddy, the banks were raw and red and the wind was harsh. We saw practically no people for days. Finally the boat whistled, and as we came around a bend, we saw a small landing with people waiting beside it. They waved and cheered as we approached. They looked tiny, like fragile beings in a threatening place." Mary shivered and turned from the window.

"Who was there to meet you?" Elizabeth asked.

"Oh, the people with children had come. The man who ran the trading post and Harry were both there, and Sam Pickett came galloping up, in his usual wild way."

"Why did you go out there if it was so bad?" asked Elizabeth.

"I was from a small town and was trained to be a schoolteacher. There were no jobs close to home, and a man I really didn't like was pressing me to marry him, but my parents rather liked him. They felt that he was safe and reliable. The thought of him made me feel like I was suffocating. Then the teacher's school I had attended wrote me with the offer to go West. I had a romanticized view of what it was like, I suppose. The offer seemed like a God-send, a way out of a situation where I knew I would be unhappy."

"Didn't you like the West at all?" Elizabeth wanted to know.

"Oh, there were certain days when the natural beauty of it all came through. Days when the wind didn't blow and the flowers bloomed, and pronghorns bounded off into the distance. On days like that, I had a sense of what it might become, and why the people kept coming. And the people, they were the best part. Wonderful, strong, generous people who pulled together. They saw that I was a stranger, that I felt uneasy out there, and they did all that they could do to make me feel at home. But they never quite succeeded."

"Did you see a lot of Indians?" Elizabeth was curious.

"Oh, yes. They came to the trading post often. They had a kind of wild grandeur to them. The Crow were especially friendly. I liked them, which was ironic because of what happened later."

"What happened later?" asked Elizabeth.

Mary look at her granddaughter, trying to judge how much she could say. "Elizabeth, I'll tell you about that part later, after we've talked more about the rest of it. There were some good things out West, and I want you to know about them."

Elizabeth frowned and pursed her lips with impatience. "Well, what were the good things, then?"

"The children in my school were wonderful. Teaching them was like pouring water on wilted flowers - they responded beautifully. They were hungry for knowledge, and for information about the world back East. I loved the teaching; that was what kept me going," explained Mary.

"What about Great Uncle Harry and Sam Pickett?" Elizabeth asked pointedly.

"They were a great help to me, especially at the beginning, when I had to start the school." Mary paused. "I guess you know that Sam Pickett fell in love with me, and asked me to marry him less than a week after I had arrived."

"What did you say?" Elizabeth was anxious to hear.

"It was hard. I wanted Sam as a friend. I could never have married him, so I tried to be gentle with him. He was hard to put off, and I even told him that there was someone back east who wanted to marry me. That was true in one way, but it really was a white lie."

"What's a white lie, Grandma?" asked Elizabeth.

"A white lie is something that you say that isn't true so that you won't hurt someone's feelings," explained Elizabeth's grandmother.

"Oh," said, Elizabeth, obviously unconvinced.

"For example," said Mary, "Suppose that I bought a new hat which was very expensive, that I really loved, and then I came to your house wearing it proudly and asked you how you liked it. You didn't like it, but to keep me from being embarrassed, you said that you did like it... that's a white lie."

Elizabeth smiled up at her grandmother. "I wouldn't do that. I'd say something about the hat needing a red feather or something. That way you'd know I thought that there was room for improvement."

Mary laughed. "You're much wiser than I was, Elizabeth."

"How did Great Uncle Harry feel about you?" Elizabeth asked.

Mary turned away. "He never said much about his feelings. I know he liked me because he helped me so much and so often. But he and Sam usually showed up together, and Sam was always talking about how he wanted to marry me. It would have been hard for Harry to have said much on that same topic without making it very awkward. Besides that, I truly don't know how he felt."

Elizabeth sat with her chin in her hand, frowning.

Mary rubbed her granddaughter's cheek. "Why do you worry so much about my old loves? They are buried deep in the past and forgotten."

"Great Uncle Harry still remembers, I know he does. He remembers everything about you."

"That's lovely to hear, Elizabeth. It really is."

Grandfather Frank entered the room. "What are you two girls chattering about? It's time for breakfast."

Elizabeth's grandmother took her by the hand and led her down the hall.

Chapter 20

Harry Goes West, Frank Stays Home

At breakfast, Tom looked at his grandfather and asked, "How come Great Uncle Harry went out West, and you didn't?" Tom's manner was not unfriendly, he was just deeply curious.

Grandfather Frank cleared his throat. "Well, Harry was about five years older than I was. He always loved hunting and fishing. He was restless in school, and he read everything that he could put his hand on about the West. When he was about sixteen, the local paper carried an advertisement asking young men to go out to St. Louis and join a new trading company that was being set up to do business with the Indians.

This was just what Harry wanted to do, and he asked our parents for permission. Of course, they would not give it. They wanted Harry to finish school and to go on to college. That was of no interest to Harry, and one morning he just up and left."

"You mean he ran away?" asked Tom incredulously.

"I guess you could call it that," said Grandfather Frank. "He wrote quite regularly, and we knew that he loved what he was doing, but our parents always grieved about him, almost as though he had contracted some strange illness and died. As I got older, I began to write to Harry, and in his letters to me he always urged me to come out and have a look at the West. Our mother, in particular, did not want me to go, but I finally persuaded her that, perhaps if I went out West and saw Harry, I could get him to come back. Our father's business was doing very well, particularly after the Civil War, and father wanted both of us to take over the business. So it was on that basis that I went out to see Harry. I had just finished at a business college, and was going to start work for my father, full time, in the fall."

"How did you like it, out there?" asked Elizabeth.

Grandfather Frank reached across the breakfast table and took his wife's hand. "The thing that I liked best about it was your Grandmother Mary, from the first moment I saw her. But I didn't think that I stood a chance. Sam Pickett was always talking about marrying her, and she was wearing that gold piece of his around her neck."

"How did that happen, Grandma?" asked Elizabeth immediately.

Mary blushed. "Frank, darling, that's not quite fair, the way you put it." Turning to Elizabeth, Mary withdrew her hand from her husband's. "I told you earlier how Sam pestered me about marrying him. At that time, he wore a gold piece around his neck. It was very precious to him, and he wanted me to wear it as a sort of engagement pendant. I would not accept it, but one morning I went out on my porch and there it was, hanging from a nail. Sam had gone off on a trip to see the Crow tribe, and he left me a note saying that I'd better wear it or someone would steal it if he left it behind. That was true, and so I put it around my neck."

Elizabeth took a spoonful of porridge, with a faintly disapproving look on her face. An awkward silence ensued, and the sound of knives and forks seemed to grow louder.

Mrs. Corliss smiled at her mother. "Elizabeth has very high standards, mother."

"I can see that," said Mary. "Elizabeth, I was not leading Sam on. I couldn't get him to take the coin back, so I continued to wear it. And it was lovely".

"As they say, money is the root of all evil!" said Grandfather Frank.

"Frank, really, that's not a helpful comment," said Mary, sharply.

Grandfather Frank was crestfallen. "I was only thinking that it was the same coin that had helped to start the trouble with that crazy Crow Indian."

"Well, then, why don't you tell your grandchildren that awful story? I certainly have no wish to." Mary rose abruptly from the table and left the room.

Grandfather Frank spread his hands imploringly. "I truly didn't mean to upset you," he said to his wife.

"What happened?" asked Tom, looking sideways at his grandfather.

"Well, I'll at least tell you my version of it," said Grandfather. Sitting back in his chair, he put his hand over his eyes and began his story.

Chapter 21

An Ugly Visit from Big Nose

On a hot July afternoon, the Renick brothers were stacking recently-arrived calico cloth in the storeroom of the trading post. The only light in the room came from the open door. The room smelled of tobacco, coffee and rancid bacon. The brothers worked silently, lifting the heavy bolts of cloth onto shelves behind the counter, which ran the length of the room. Suddenly, the light in the room faded. Both men turned and saw the silhouette of a tall Indian in the doorway. Harry stepped forward and made the sign of peace, and spoke a short phrase of greeting in the Crow tongue. The Indian made no response. Frank became nervous as he looked at the silent Indian, whose face he could not see. The warrior cradled a rifle in his left arm, and was dressed in leggings and moccasins. His chest and shoulders were massive. "Who is he? What does he want?" asked Frank.

"I can't see," said Harry, stooping to lift a kerosene lamp from behind the counter. "Be careful, I smell whiskey," he added, as he struck a match.

The lamp flared, and the shadows were driven back to the corners of the room. The Renick brothers stared at the Indian, who stood silently. The warrior moved forward, closer to the light. Harry noticed that he walked with a slight limp. "It's Big Nose," Harry said out of the side of his mouth. "He's very dangerous."

Big Nose stood at the counter. He glowered at Harry, his eyes narrowed and glittering. "Whiskey," he demanded.

Harry spread his hands, palms upward, and then made the sign for empty. Big Nose swung his rifle so that it pointed directly at Harry's stomach. He cocked the rifle, and the sharp double click seemed to reverberate through the store room. "Whiskey," he demanded again, this time in a louder voice.

"Do you have any?" asked Frank in a high-pitched voice.

"No, we don't sell whiskey," said Harry. "He knows that. He's here to make trouble."

Harry turned slowly and took a small package of tobacco off a shelf in back of the counter. He placed it in front of Big Nose, who knocked it disdainfully aside with the barrel of his rifle. He jabbed Harry in the pit of the stomach with the rifle, and laughed harshly as Harry grunted in pain.

"You stop that!" Frank said, his voice cracking with tension.

Big Nose lifted the rifle to his shoulder, and pointed it at Frank's face. His finger was on the trigger. The three men stood as if frozen.

Mary Atherton walked suddenly into the storeroom. Big Nose heard her step at the door, and swung his rifle toward her. Totally surprised at the scene before her, Mary stepped back against the wall, one hand at her chest.

Big Nose lowered his rifle, and started toward Mary. Her copper hair shone in the lamp light, and her eyes were wide with fear. Big Nose moved toward her, his eyes fixed on her face. He leaned to one side to look at Mary from another angle. She felt the impact of his eyes, and a deep flush spread over her face. She nervously twisted the thong around her neck on which the double eagle hung. Big Nose reached out and took the double eagle in his hand. He looked at it intently. Turning to Harry, he asked in a harsh tone, "Is this the woman of Red Beard?"

Mary pulled the coin from Big Nose's grasp. "I'm no one's woman. I teach school here," she said defiantly.

Big Nose's eyes narrowed. "I know that gold piece, it has the mark of Broken Lance; it belongs to Red

Beard. You are his woman." With a laugh, he strode from the room.

Frank moved toward the door. "Wait, stay back," snapped Harry. As he spoke, a rifle boomed and a heavy slug struck the door frame, at head height. Harry seized a pistol from behind the counter, and lunged out the door in time to see Big Nose, on a great pinto stallion, gallop through the gate of the trading post. His wild cry came back to them, over the log stockade.

Mary was ashen, and her voice trembled. "What does he mean, Harry, what does he mean?"

Harry looked at Frank, afraid to answer.

Chapter 22

An Eagle Takes a Squirrel

Elizabeth rose quickly from her chair, ran out of the living room and up the stairs to her grandmother's room. The door was open, and she saw Mary sitting on the edge of the bed, with her head bowed. Elizabeth threw herself into her grandmother's arms. "I hate that story, it's awful, I don't want to hear it," she cried.

Mary Renick stroked Elizabeth's hair and held her close. Elizabeth rubbed her nose with the back of her hand and sniffed loudly. Lifting her tear-streaked face she said, "Grandma, please tell me gently what happened. I want to know, but..." Her voice trailed off.

"I know, dear, I know what you mean." Mary cleared her throat and took up the story. "Big Nose was a fierce Indian who hated all white men. He hated Sam Pickett especially, because Sam had broken a bone in Big Nose's leg that hadn't healed properly, so he walked with a limp and could no longer run fast. He had tried for a long time to catch up with Sam, but he hadn't been able to. Big Nose was one of only a few Crow Indians who wanted to fight the white man; most of them wanted to be at peace. Big Nose was given whiskey by some bad traders, and that made him worse. So the day he came into the trading post and saw me with Sam's double eagle around my neck, he thought he had a way to get to Sam."

Mary looked down at Elizabeth, whose face was pressed against her. "Are you all right, Elizabeth? Shall I go on?"

"Yes," said Elizabeth in a small voice.

"After that, Sam and Harry seemed to know what Big Nose had in mind, so they both watched me carefully. I slept inside the trading post stockade and never went anywhere alone. That was very confining, and I grew restless. One beautiful summer morning, I decided to walk down to the stream that ran close to the trading post. There were blue and orange flowers that grew there, and I wanted something to brighten the drabness of my room. I thought I was being very alert as I walked to the stream. I knew I was doing something that Sam and Harry had forbidden me to do, and suddenly, out of nowhere, there was Big

Nose on his huge pinto horse. He leaned down and swooped me up like an eagle taking a squirrel. I struggled, but it was no use. His arm was as hard as a tree-branch. We rode for about a mile, with me slung across the saddle in front of him. We stopped in a grove of trees where another Indian waited. Big Nose lifted me down, quite politely, and spoke to me for the first time. He said, "You be quiet. I will not hurt you!"

"Big Nose saw that I was still wearing the double eagle. He smiled when he saw it, and took it from around my neck. The thong loosened my hairpins, and my hair came down. I remember that he reached out and touched my hair. It was quite lovely in those days." Mary paused. "Then he gave the double eagle to the other Indian and said something in Crow. The Indian rode off, in the direction of the trading post. Big Nose tied his horse at the edge of the grove of trees, where it could be easily seen. Then he led me away from the trees, to the top of a low ridge, where there was heavy brush and some rocks. His rifle was already there, so I knew that he had everything planned. He thought that Sam would come right after me, and he planned to ambush him and shoot him from behind those rocks."

"Did Sam come to save you?" asked Elizabeth, in a frightened voice.

"Of course he did, bless his heart," said Mary, smiling in remembrance. "And dear Harry was right with him. Big Nose had tied me up, and put a strip of cloth over my mouth, so that I couldn't scream. He lay behind the brush and the rocks, with his rifle. He had a perfect shot at anyone coming from the trading post. I twisted around so that I could see. We lay there for what seemed like a long time, and then I heard Big Nose grunt. Straining my eyes, I saw what looked like five horsemen come into view. I first recognized Sam, because he was so tall, and then I saw Harry. The other three were Indians. They stopped while they were still out of range of Big Nose's rifle. I saw Sam point, and I knew that they had seen Big Nose's horse. The three Indians turned back and disappeared.

Sam and Harry waited for a few minutes, which seemed to me like forever, and then began to ride forward. Sam was in the lead. I had been slowly inching my way closer to Big Nose, and I had gotten to a point where, if I swung my legs, I thought that I could push his feet out from under him. I watched as he sighted down the rifle. When I heard him cock it, I threw myself toward him. My legs came down on top of his feet as I heard the gun fire. He turned to me. I have never seen such rage on anyone's face. I knew then that he'd missed Sam. He leapt to his feet and grabbed me by my hair. He swung me in front of him as a shield and pointed his rifle at Sam, who was galloping toward us. Big Nose shouted something, and Sam pulled up his horse. Big Nose shouted again, and Sam dropped his gun and raised his hands. Harry, who was a little behind Sam, did the same. Big Nose shouted again, and Sam began to ride slowly forward, his hands in the air. Big Nose was holding his rifle with one hand, and I knew he wanted Sam to come closer so that he wouldn't miss him - he was going to shoot him dead. Sam rode forward. I'll never forget it, he wore such a calm expression." Mary's voice broke and she rubbed her eyes.

"I was struggling, trying to make it harder for Big Nose to shoot. Sam spoke to me, 'Don't struggle, Mary, he said that he won't hurt you.' Sam's voice was calm, and he smiled at me as he spoke."

Mary sighed and felt Elizabeth trembling in her arms. "Big Nose cocked the rifle, and I knew that he was about to shoot. Suddenly there was a strange sound, a sort of whoosh, and Big Nose lurched against me. He let go of me and whirled around. As I fell to the ground, I saw other Indians on horseback. Big Nose had the shaft of an arrow sticking out of his back. I almost fainted."

Elizabeth looked up. "What happened next, Grandma?"

"The other Indians fought Big Nose and he was killed."

"So the others were good Indians, helping Sam and Great Uncle Harry?"

"Yes, they were. They saved our lives, but I never got to thank them. They rode away, taking Big Nose's body with them."

Frank Renick stepped quietly into the room, and looked at his wife and his granddaughter, clinging to each other as memories of that terrible day washed over them. Mary saw her husband and reached toward him. "I'll never forget the expression on your face as you drove up with that wagon. I knew then that you loved me, and I knew that you would take me away from that wild place."

"I followed after Sam and Harry as fast as I could. There was a wagon hitched up and I borrowed it," he said a little defensively.

"That wagon felt like a queen's chariot to me, as we drove back," said Mary with a smile.

Elizabeth had a thousand questions to ask, but didn't know which one to start with. She frowned and her grandmother noticed.

"What is it, Elizabeth?"

"Oh, I was thinking about Sam and Great Uncle Harry. They saved you, and then they lost you."

Chapter 23

Suitcases and Memories

Elizabeth was coming home from school during a gentle April rain. A determined, small figure in a yellow slicker, she moved with purposeful steps through the greens and grays of the wet spring day. Elizabeth walked with her head down and her brow furrowed. She had decided that the one thing she needed to know more about was what had happened to Sam Pickett after Mary returned east with Frank. She looked up at the sky. It promised unrelenting rain and, with a sigh, Elizabeth went inside.

Mrs. Corliss was waiting for Elizabeth in the front hall and greeted her with a hug. "Where's Grandma?" asked Elizabeth, getting down to business.

"She's upstairs, packing," said her mother. "She's depressed, as she always is when she has to fit all those things she didn't use back into suitcases that don't seem to hold as much as they did before. Take her a cup of tea, you'll cheer her up."

Elizabeth carefully carried a cup of tea to her grandmother's room. She knocked on the door which stood slightly ajar. Her grandmother immediately pulled the door open, brushing a wisp of hair from her forehead. Behind her, piles of clothes lay between open trunks and suitcases. It was a scene of chaos and disarray.

"Hello, Grandma, can I help you?" asked Elizabeth.

"Oh, come in dear. I always make such a mess when I'm packing," said Mary.

"I brought you some tea; it will help you get organized," said Elizabeth.

"I need something," said Mary. She was grateful for any excuse to interrupt her struggles with her wardrobe and the trunks that seemed to be too few and too small. Sitting on a corner of the bed, Mary looked at her granddaughter. "Elizabeth, I sense that you have something on your mind. What's on your mind, my dear? I hate the thought of going off tomorrow, we've had such good talks, you and I."

Elizabeth scratched her nose. "I guess I'm not sure what happened to Sam Pickett. Can you tell me again what you heard?"

Mary took a sip of tea before answering. "The truth is, I don't know. When I told Harry and Sam that I was going back east to marry Frank, their reactions were different. Harry was sad, but Sam seemed wounded. It was a terrible time for me. I hated to hurt anyone, but I knew that I could never live for very long in the West, and that if I tried, I would make everyone around me miserable. Harry seemed to understand that, but Sam just looked bewildered and terribly gloomy. Harry came to the steamboat landing to see us off, but Sam didn't appear. I had been trying to return the double eagle to Sam, but he wouldn't take it. At the landing, I took it out of my purse and gave it to Harry. He looked at me with that wonderful grin of his, and said, "I'll pass it along, but not right away." And so I left, holding Frank's hand, watching the small figures on the landing as we pulled away. At the last minute, a man rode up on the top of the ridge overlooking the landing. I was sure it was Sam, but he wouldn't wave, and sat, slumped in the saddle until we lost sight of him." Mary lowered her head and brushed her eyes with the back of her hand, "That was such a hard thing for me to do, and yet I had to. I had to leave. You understand that, don't you?" she asked, plaintively.

Elizabeth suddenly felt far older than she had ever felt before. She hugged her grandmother and said, "Of course I do."

Mary sniffed and laughed. "I always get depressed when I have to pack, and talking about leaving the West is always sad for me. It brings back a sense of failure. And yet, I've had a wonderful life with Frank, the life I was meant to lead."

"When you got back east, what did you hear about Sam?" asked Elizabeth.

"Well, Harry wrote quite regularly, but I only got one letter from Sam," Mary answered.

"What did Sam's letter say?" asked Elizabeth.

"It wasn't very long, and it didn't speak of any of his feelings. I remember it was about 'moving on', that was the phrase he used. He spoke of going to the Southwest, where the winters were warmer. That's about all I remember. I think I still have the letter somewhere up in the attic."

"Will you send it to me if you find it?" asked Elizabeth.

"Of course I will. But I haven't seen it for years," said Mary.

Elizabeth pursed her lips and nodded her head. "I'd like to see it," she said. "What were Great Uncle Harry's letters like?"

"Oh, they were always funny and lighthearted. Harry always seemed to be able to tell a story about himself that would make me smile. He would tell me about falling off a horse or losing at poker. He had a wonderful eye, and his letters always painted pictures in my mind. I loved hearing from him. He hasn't written much in the last few years. Always at Christmas something will come from him, but not much besides that," said Mary.

"Did Harry ever hear from Sam once he left?" asked Elizabeth.

"Only once that I can remember," said Mary. "Harry spoke of Sam's liking the Southwest, and he said that one day he'd likely follow Sam, when the winters got too cold." Mary's voice trailed off, and there was silence.

Finally, Elizabeth asked the inevitable question, "Do you think that Sam is dead?"

"I don't know, Elizabeth. He may be, or he may be alive and well in some warm and friendly place in Arizona or New Mexico."

"I should have asked Great Uncle Harry about Sam, but I didn't," said Elizabeth shaking her head.

Mrs. Corliss entered the room. Looking at the two pensive figures sitting in front of her, she said, "I think we'd better get your packing done, Mother. Your train leaves quite early in the morning."

And so, reluctantly, the three of them turned to the task of putting clothes in trunks. A visit was coming to an end.

Chapter 24

A Home in the Desert

May 1, 1923

Dear Great Uncle Harry,

How are you? I am fine. Thank you for the silver dollars under my plate at Christmas. I am sorry that I have not written before to thank you. I don't think that Tom has written you, either; at least I'm doing better at that than he is.

Grandma Mary and Grandfather Frank were here for a visit. It was fun. We talked a lot about the old days in the West. I don't think that Grandma would have been happy out West, but she was sorry to say good-bye to you and Sam. What has happened to Sam? Is he dead?

Much love,
Elizabeth

* * * * * *

July 4, 1923

Dear Elizabeth,

All of the boys are in town whooping it up for the Glorious Fourth, which gives me a good chance to write to you.

Thank you for your letter telling me about Mary's visit. I am always glad to have word of her. I agree with you that she would not have been happy out West, at least the way it was when she left. Things got better after the Indian Wars were over, but she couldn't have known that in advance.

You ask about Sam. After Mary left, he was not the same. He grew apart from his friends and got into some trouble along the way. I could sense that he was getting restless, and finally he came to me and said that he was going to head out toward the Southwest. He left the next day. I missed him at the trading post; he and I had a lot of experiences together. Sam wrote me a few letters. He always tried to sound cheerful, but I'm not sure that he was. He seemed to be moving around a lot; each letter came from a different place.

At one time, he was working at a trading post in Navajo country. Another time, he was working at a dude ranch. I haven't heard from Sam for four or five years now, but I think he's doing all right. Somehow I believe that I'd have heard if he wasn't.

It's taking me longer than I thought it would to civilize this old place enough so that you and Tom can enjoy it. This summer I'll add a kitchen to the back. That will mean that we'll have to hire a better cook, which will help all of us.

Your little filly is growing up fine, and by the time I have this place fixed up, she'll be ready to ride.

I hope you have a good summer.

Love,
Great Uncle Harry

* * * * * *

September 15, 1923

Dear Great Uncle Harry,

Thank you for your letter. I had a good summer. I took lessons at Miss Hackworth's stable. I can ride better than I could before. Sometimes I ask her to let me ride on that Western saddle you used - it is a lot easier! Miss Hackworth has sold Saladin, who got wild. She said that you were the last person to be able to handle him.

You will be interested to know that that rude horse who made the awful noises is still there. She was fine all summer except for one day. That day, a pretty girl came with her boyfriend. The girl rode the bad horse. It made those noises as soon as she began to trot. Her boyfriend tried not to laugh, but he couldn't help it. (I couldn't either.) The girl got mad and got off the horse. She threw her boyfriend's hat and coat into the watering trough, and drove off in his car. I felt sorry for them, but I still had to giggle.

Thank you for telling me about Sam. I wonder about him a lot. I hope he is all right. Please let me know if you hear from him. Tom and I are looking forward to visiting you when your ranch is ready. Tom is trying to play football on the school team, but I don't think he is doing too well. He has a girlfriend.

Have a good winter.

Much love,
Elizabeth

* * * * * *

February 15, 1924

Dear Elizabeth,

Thank you for your happy letter. I'm glad that you are enjoying those old silver dollars. It was my great pleasure to give them to you.

We have been having a very cold winter, and I have been inside more than usual. I was poking around in an old saddlebag, and I found the last letter that Sam wrote to me. It's older than I thought. Time flies. I'm sending you Sam's letter to keep. It shows his flavor. He was an original. I'm glad that I knew him.

The new kitchen works fine; now to find a cook who can stand being out here with us old hound dogs! My projects for this summer are to build you a bedroom on the second floor, and to improve the road to the ranch so that we can drive out here. I plan to get a motor car this spring, and will have Buck, the wrangler and soon to be ex-cook, learn to drive. That way, you and Tom can arrive in style.

I'd say that we'll be ready for you both by mid-June of next year. Write it down and don't forget. I'll send railroad tickets when its time.

I'm looking forward to your visit.

Love,
Great Uncle Harry

* * * * * *

General Delivery
Tombstone, Arizona
23 October 1915

Dear Harry,

Well, I'm now in Arizona, in a town that's not as tough as it was, but then, neither am I. They made this part of the West a state three years ago. I'm not sure why they bothered. People seem about the same, just more taxes to complain about, and more rules. A man can hardly spit without having somebody complain. Things aren't what they was.

I've been doing some wrangling, some bar-tending and some work at a dude ranch that's hard to describe. The easterners who come here have a romantic view of what the "Old West" was like. They look for it all over the place, but when they run into something that's really like the way things was - like a rattlesnake or a sandstorm, they come down with a case of the fantods quicker than you can spit.

At the ranch, I'm known as the great Indian fighter, and after dinner around the camp fire, I'm supposed to tell my stories of how I won the West. I'm glad you're not here to listen, you'd

Sam Pickett - 1915 in Tombstone

die laughing. You would not recognize anyone in the stories I tell, including me. I wiped out the whole Sioux tribe single-handedly, and drove Geronimo to surrender. It goes great around the campfire and it pays the rent, so I guess I can't complain.

I often think of the old days. I wonder how Mary is, but I guess I'll never know. I think I'll stay here a while, I kind of like it. Drop me a line if you can.

Your old friend,
Sam

* * * * * *

To:
General Delivery
Tombstone, Arizona

February 25, 1924

Dear Mr. Pickett,

My name is Elizabeth Corliss, and I am Mary Atherton's granddaughter. I have heard about you from my Great Uncle, Harry Renick and from Grandma. I am eleven years old, and I have a brother Tom. He is almost 15.

I am writing to you to thank you for saving Grandma when Big Nose took her away. You were very brave. I also admire you for not killing No Feathers, and for being friends with the Crow, they sound like good people. I am going out to visit Great Uncle Harry in the summer of next year. He lives on his ranch near Parkman, Wyoming. If Tombstone is not too far, why don't you come to the ranch when I am there? I would like to meet you and thank you in person.

My Grandma still remembers you well. It was hard for her to leave the West, but she has been happy in Boston. She is very grateful to you, and so am I.

I am writing this to General Delivery at Tombstone. I hope you are still there, even though it has been ten years since your last letter to Great Uncle Harry. Please let me hear from you.

Sincerely,
Elizabeth Corliss

* * * * * *

June 25, 1925

Dear Miss Corliss,

My name is Helen Higginbotham, and I am the postmistress of Tombstone, Arizona. I was appointed to my position last fall. On my first day on the job, I found a dusty packet of letters stuck away in a corner. They were letters sent to General Delivery, never claimed. The previous postmaster never made any effort to see that those letters were delivered. I determined to do better, in the interest of improving government services to the citizens of this, our newest state. Over time, I was able to locate people and deliver all of the letters except for yours. I would have returned your letter, except that the local people said that they had heard of Sam Pickett as someone who drifted through town from time to time. I kept hoping and asking questions.

Last week, a cowboy came into the post office and said that he thought that I could find Sam Pickett at the livery stable. I walked over on my lunch hour, with your letter in my hand. The stable seemed quite deserted at first, but I went in. As I looked around, a very tall old man walked in, carrying a bag of supplies. I asked him if he was Sam Pickett, and he replied, "I used to be, and I guess I still am."

I told Mr. Pickett that I had a letter for him, and he seemed quite surprised. He asked who it was from. I read him your name, and he shook his head, as he did not know who you were. I handed him the letter, and we walked out of the dark stable into the sunlight. Mr. Pickett was tall, as I said, with a beard that was white, with a few traces of red still remaining. He was quite thin, and had pale blue eyes. He was dressed as I have seen many men of the desert dress: a faded red shirt, with patched gray trousers and stout boots. He looked like a man with an interesting past.

Mr. Pickett opened your letter and tried to read it. He squinted hard at your writing, which I thought was very neat and legible. Then, embarrassed, he asked me to read it to him. He said something about having broken his glasses. I believed him, for he did not seem to be the illiterate type.

I read your letter, and as I did, a wonderful smile spread over his face. He asked me to read the letter again, and I was glad to do so. He said, "That letter is worth its weight in gold to me." He did a shuffle dance in the dust of the main street, just out of pure joy. Then he rushed back into the stable and came out with a magnifying glass. Using that, he was able to read your letter. As he read it, he had the most beatific expression on his face. He folded the letter and put it carefully in his pocket. He reached into another vest pocket, and pulled out a small leather pouch. From that pouch, he took a gold nugget, which he gave to me. He thanked me for taking the trouble to find him (he had noticed the date on the letter, which was more than a year ago), and asked me to write to you. He said, "I haven't got time to write right now, as there is gold out in the desert waiting to be discovered." He laughed as he said it. Then he turned serious, and asked me to remember what he said. I had a pencil in my bag, so I wrote down his words, exactly as he said them. This is what he said, "Thank Elizabeth for writing, and for remembering me. Tell her that I have found a home in the desert, and that I am all right. When she visits Harry Renick, she should tell him that. He should come and visit me here, when the Wyoming winters get too cold. Finally, when she writes to her Grandma, give her my love, and tell her that I'm glad that she has been happy." With that, he turned away and blew his nose in a big red handkerchief.

I shook hands with Mr. Pickett, and thanked him for the gold nugget, which has turned out to be quite valuable. I am using the proceeds to improve the quality of the post office.

I walked back from the stable with a full heart, thinking that, in this case, I had been able to do something significant by delivering that letter. Later that afternoon, I saw Mr. Pickett pass by on his way out of town. He was riding a mule, and leading two others who were heavily laden. I went out on the porch and waved. Mr. Pickett swept off his hat, in quite a gallant gesture, and called out, "Thank you, again."

I watched him as he rode out of town. He is an enduring figure, and I can see how he did those wonderful things that you mentioned in your letter. I take great satisfaction in sending you this news.

Yours very truly,
Helen Higginbotham

* * * * * *

This letter arrived just a few days before Elizabeth and Tom caught the train to visit Great Uncle Harry. Elizabeth took the letter with her.

Elizabeth and the horse of her dreams

Glossary of Terms

Counting Coup *(page 34)*

A term usually associated with warfare between the Indian tribes of the Great Plains. Chief Plenty Coups, a renowned war chief of the Crow tribe, once described the ultimate coup as slapping the face of an armed enemy who is attacking you with a knife or war club, and escaping unharmed.

A coup stick was not a weapon, but an implement to be used in counting coup on an armed, threatening enemy, as No Feathers does with Sam Pickett. The warrior's courage is demonstrated by counting coup, and his enemy is left unharmed, but impressed or even shamed by the demonstration of his enemy's bravery.

The Fantods *(pages 59, 128)*

Mark Twain was fond of this humorous reference to an uneasy feeling of apprehension, caused perhaps by the sudden appearance of a snake or the bizarre behavior of a stranger. In one case, Twain had Huckleberry Finn refer negatively to a series of pictures which "gave him the fantods". From my own college days, I remember having a terrible case of the fantods as I approached an examination on a book that I had not read thoroughly enough; I think I got a D on the test. The fantods were justified.

Parfleche *(pages 31, 32, 34, 37)*

An often-ornamented carrying case made of animal hide, used to transport precious personal belongings or pemmican.

Pemmican *(pages 31, 34, 38)*

Plains Indians trail rations made of dried beef, cut into very small pieces, mixed with animal fat and assorted wild berries. In 1952, I was subjected to three weeks of arctic survival training, and pemmican was what I carried along to eat. If you are hungry enough, even pemmican tastes good.

About the Author

Donald Gregg's first pair of shoes were moccasins, made by the Sioux. He has had a lifelong interest in Native Americans of the northern plains, particularly the Crow and the Blackfeet. His grandfather, Harry Renick Gregg, (1852-1950), told him many stories of the Old West, and of seeing Abraham Lincoln's funeral train, as a boy of twelve. Great Uncle Harry embodies him in this book.

Gregg wrote the first draft of this book in 1989, while awaiting Senate confirmation to become U.S. Ambassador to South Korea, where he served, 1989-93.

In 2014, Gregg's memoir, *Pot Shards, Fragments of a Life Lived in CIA, the White House, and the Two Koreas*, was published by New Academia Publishing in Washington, D. C.

CPSIA information can be obtained
at www.ICGtesting.com
Printed in the USA
LVOW06s0222281116
514711LV00028B/1446/P